BEASTS OF OLYMPUS

ZEUS'S EAGLE

Lucy Coats is the author of more than thirty books for readers of all ages, including *Atticus the Storyteller's 100 Greek Myths*, which was shortlisted for the Blue Peter Book Award. She began her storytelling career as a bookseller, editor and journalist, and has been fascinated by myths and legends ever since she can remember. She lives in deepest south Northamptonshire with her husband and three unruly dogs. When she is not writing, she cooks, grows vegetables and sits in her stone circle, looking at the stars.

Also available:

BEAST KEEPER
HOUND OF HADES
STEEDS OF THE GODS
DRAGON HEALER
CENTAUR SCHOOL

BEASTS OF OLYMPUS

ZEUS'S EAGLE

LUCY COATS

with illustrations by
David Roberts

Piccadilly
PRESS

First published in Great Britain in 2016 by
Piccadilly Press
80-81 Wimpole Street, London, W1G 9RE
www.piccadillypress.co.uk

A CIP catalogue record for this book
is available from the British Library.

ISBN: 978–1–848–12531–5
also available as an ebook

Typeset by Palimpsest Book Production Limited,
Falkirk, Stirlingshire
Printed and bound by Clays Ltd, St Ives plc

MIX
Paper from
responsible sources
FSC® C018072
www.fsc.org

Piccadilly Press is an imprint of Bonnier Zaffre,
a Bonnier Publishing Company
www.bonnierpublishing.co.uk

For DB, who had eagles in his daydreams and
diamonds in his eyes

1

MAD MAENADS

The little pegasus's wings flapped slower and slower as he flew over the sea. The smell of salt filled Demon's nostrils, and gentle waves splashed and rippled below him. The water was so clear that he could even see tiny shoals of fish darting across the seabed. The sharp peaks of Mount Pelion cut into the pale pinkish-blue dawn sky ahead, with tiny coves and beaches of blinding white sand strung at its feet like a necklace.

'Come on, Keith,' Demon said, patting the

winged horse's shiny black neck. 'Only a little further. You can do it.' But poor Keith had no breath to spare for even a small whinny. He spread his wings wide and began to glide downwards, lower and lower, until Demon's toes were nearly skimming the water.

'Hey!' shouted a familiar voice. 'Watch those big feet of yours!' Demon looked down. There was his friend Eunice the nereid, King Poseidon's Official Handmaid to the Hippocamps and Damsel to the Dolphins, surrounded by her dolphin charges, and riding her own dolphin steed, Seapetal. But Demon had no time to greet her. Keith's wings gave one last weak flap and he collapsed into the water.

'Help!' Demon scrambled off Keith's back as he started to sink, trying to hold the small beast up and swim at the same time. Then a wave hit them. Demon swallowed a big gulp of seawater and began to choke and thrash, letting go of Keith. Why couldn't he breathe? Had Poseidon's spell for keeping him alive underwater worn off?

Almost immediately a sleek dolphin body lifted him up.

'Seawhistle!' he spluttered, clutching frantically at its big fin as water and snot ran out of his nose and down his chin in slimy streams. Demon didn't care how disgusting he looked, though.

'S-save K-Keith,' he gargled. He needn't have worried. Eunice already had things under control. Two dolphins were under Keith's wings, swimming him to shore. As soon as the winged horse felt the land under his hooves he staggered up onto the sandy beach and collapsed again, whinnying pathetically. Eunice and Demon were not far behind, and as Eunice stumbled towards Keith on her flipper feet, Demon managed to wheeze out a brief *thank you* before he fell to his knees beside the little pegasus's head, stroking him behind the ears and making soothing sounds, before unknotting the sacks that were tied to him. Demon peered anxiously inside them. Luckily nothing had been damaged by the seawater – including the precious notebook Athena had given him as a reward for curing the phoenix, the ball of fire ant nectar and the priceless phoenix feather.

'Where in all the world's oceans have you come from?' Eunice asked. 'And what were you doing flying over the sea? If you needed transport I could have taken you in Poseidon's chariot. He trusts me to drive it on my own now, you know,' she added in a proud voice.

'Long story,' said Demon. 'Tell you in a minute. Right now I need to get some sandflowers out of my sack for Keith here.' Reaching in, he pulled out a handful of damp yellow blooms. 'Come on, Keith,' he said, holding them out. 'Have a few of these and you'll soon feel better.'

A soft, black nose nuzzled at his palm, and the flowers disappeared one by one.

'Yummy scrum,' Keith neighed, scrambling upright and shaking himself in a flurry of sand and feathery wings. He nudged the sack. 'More,' he demanded. While he was munching, Demon sat on the beach and told Eunice all about his adventures with Antaeus the giant, about saving the phoenix from the fire devils and about his friend Prince Peleus's surprising alliance with the enormous Myrmex fire ants.

'Oh – and I'm also Apprentice Healer to Chiron,' he added, trying not to sound boastful. 'The centaur god, you know?'

Eunice's eyes got rounder and rounder.

'You are lucky,' she said. 'I love my new job, but since you left Poseidon's realm, nothing exciting has happened – well, apart from my sister Thetis falling in love with some human prince she saw walking on the island of Aegina. Now he's disappeared, and she swears she'll never be happy till she finds him again and he marries her. She's cried so much that she made the sea even saltier.' Eunice snorted. 'If it makes a person that dopey and silly, I'll *never* fall in love.'

Demon frowned.

'My friend Peleus comes from Aegina, and he's a prince. But it couldn't be him, could it? He's far too young to be thinking about getting married. Anyway, he's still in the Mountains of Burning Sand, taking wrestling lessons from Antaeus. I had to leave him behind with Keith's daughter, Sky Pearl.' Suddenly he yawned, his mouth gaping wider than a whale's. 'Sorry, Eunice – I've been flying for two whole days and nights. I've . . . I've . . .' Demon's eyelids drooped, his head nodded onto his chest, and soon he was snoring.

When Demon awoke, Helios's chariot was halfway up the sky, and Eunice and Keith were asleep beside him. There was no sign of the dolphins.

'Oh no!' Demon groaned, leaping to his feet. 'Wake up, everyone! I've got to get back to Chiron's cave. Hermes only knows what's happened there while I've been away.' He didn't even want to think about what might be happening in the Stables of the Gods up on Olympus. He'd been worrying about Arnie the Griffin and his purple spots all the way back from the phoenix's cave. What if the beast's feathers were still dropping out?

'I've got to get back too,' Eunice said. 'It's nearly the hippocamps' feeding time! Come and see me soon.'

'I will,' Demon said. 'And thank you for rescuing us.'

'Anytime,' she called, whistling for Seapetal as she dived into the sea and disappeared beneath the waves.

Outside Chiron's cave was a small crowd of girls, dressed in an assortment of ragged animal skins, with wreaths of ivy and berries on their heads. Each carried a leafy staff with a pine cone on top, and they were huddled round someone or something lying in the shadow of a large rock. Just as Keith was about to land, he saw them, let out a single panicky neigh and reared in the air, tipping Demon and the sacks off and over his hindquarters. They landed on the ground with a thump.

'MAENADS!' Keith whinnied, wings fluttering frantically. 'Run awayheyey, Demon, run away fast!'

But Demon had no breath to run away. He lay there, wheezing and trying to catch his breath, as the girls sprinted over to him, letting out wild shrieks and yells. They picked him up, one girl to each leg and arm, and whirled him round and round, howling like mad wolves, till he felt sick and dizzy as well as breathless.

'Stop!' he croaked. 'Put me down! Don't tread on the sacks!'

'But we're having such fun,' said one of the girls, as the rest shrieked with laughter.

'Well, I'm not!' Demon began to struggle, but it was no good. Now they were throwing him up in the air and catching him. The sky and the rocks twisted and turned, till he didn't know which way was up. Then he heard a loud groan.

'My stomach!' said a trembling voice. 'My poor stomach.' Immediately, the girls dumped Demon unceremoniously on the grass, and rushed over to the figure by the rock.

'Poor old Nicey,' they cooed. 'Chiron will be back in a bit. Just lie still. You'll be better soon.'

Demon crawled away and was quietly sick behind a tree. Wiping his mouth, he stood up, feeling rather wobbly. But Chiron clearly wasn't here, and there was a patient to treat, so he stowed the sacks safely behind a big stone and tottered over to the little group to see if he could help.

As soon as he saw who was lying on the ground, though, his heart sank straight down to his toes.

It was Dionysus, the god of parties, and he didn't look at all good. His face was the colour of sour cream mixed with an unhealthy green glow, and his wreath of grapes and vine leaves drooped over one red-rimmed eye. Demon had only treated one god before, and that was his dad, Pan, for a headache. This looked much more serious. What would those girls do to him if he didn't cure their precious god? He'd heard of the maenads before. They had a nasty reputation for tearing people to pieces. Demon started to tiptoe away backwards, but it was too late. He'd been noticed.

'Hey,' said one of the girls, showing teeth that were pointed and stained with red. 'Where do you think you're going, little shrimp?' She advanced, graceful as a stalking cat, sharp-nailed fingers stretched out towards him like human claws.

Demon took Keith's advice and began to run.

Screaming delightedly, the girls gave chase.

Demon dodged through the trees, panting with fear, breath catching in his throat as his legs began to slow. Now he knew what prey felt like when it was being chased, and he didn't like it one little bit. He could almost feel the mad maenads' breath on the back of his neck. Was this really how he was going to die? Frantically, he looked back over his shoulder. They were almost on him!

'OOF!' He ran into something solid and warm and hairy.

'What's all this?' thundered a familiar voice above him, as Demon ducked under a gigantic horse belly. 'Stop this nonsense at once, girls.'

It was Chiron the centaur god, and in his arms he was holding something that squalled like a herd of hurt hippogriffs. Joined with the shrieks of the maenads, it made a truly infernal racket.

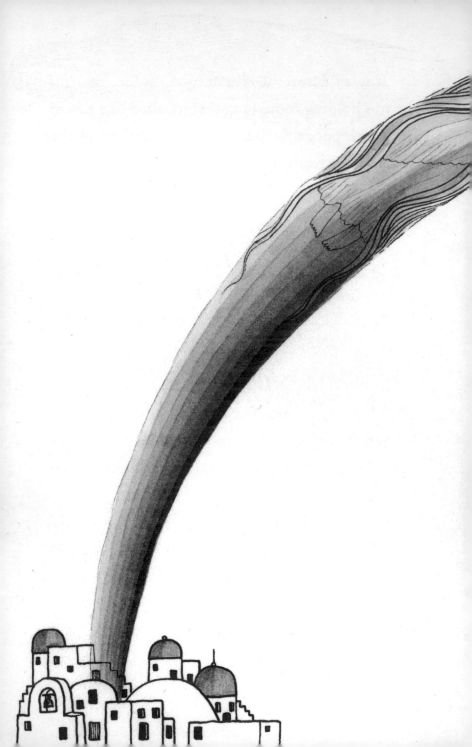

2

THE NOISY BABY

The good thing was that Chiron had returned, so Demon was now safe. The bad thing was that the squirming, squawking bundle his teacher held reeked of poo.

'Here,' the centaur god said, bending down and shoving the bundle into Demon's arms, along with a leather bottle and a bag. 'Deal with this. I'll see to the maenads.'

The squawking had turned to a high-pitched wailing. Demon wanted to cover his ears, but he had both hands full. Shoving his way past the maenads, who were now tugging at Chiron and urging him to help Dionysus, Demon put everything down on a flat piece of grass. Cautiously he unwrapped the top end of the bundle – the bit where all the noise was coming from. A round red face glared up at him, crinkled like an angry old man's. It had very blue eyes and a tuft of black hair sticking straight up out of the top of its head.

It was a human baby.

'Hello, baby,' he said. 'Where did Chiron find you?'

Wah! howled the baby, its eyes screwing up into tear-filled slits. *Wah waaahhh waaaahhhh!*

By the time Demon had discovered clean squares of linen in the bag, unwrapped the smelly end of the bundle and mopped up the screaming child as best he could, Dionysus and his maenad girls were laughing and running back into the forest. The baby had spat out most of the liquid in the bottle, but she was limp and warm in

Demon's arms, finally asleep. Chiron nodded at him approvingly.

'Good lad,' he said. 'I can see you'll make a fine babysitter for young Hygeia here. She's a very tricky feeder. Won't drink her mum's milk, or anything from a cow, so I said I'd have her for a week or so to give Asclepius and his wife a bit of a rest. I expect it's only a bit of colic, but they were very worried about her starving.'

Demon sighed. Extra babysitting duties were the very last thing he needed right now.

'Please, Chiron,' he pleaded ten minutes later, after baby Hygeia, still sleeping peacefully, had been laid in a makeshift cradle filled with soft sheepskins. 'I promise I'll be here tomorrow, but I have to go back to Olympus right now and wake the griffin up. And before that I have to get Hestia some five-leafed panax and some bee gold so she'll give me some meat to feed the griffin with. If I don't have a proper meal for Arnie right away, it'll be so hungry that it won't just bite my finger off this time, it'll be my whole head.'

Chiron looked at him, trying not to smile.

'And just where were you going to get five-leaved panax and bee gold from, my young apprentice?' he asked. 'That's rare stuff, you know.'

Demon hung his head.

'I was hoping you'd give me some,' he said.

'Very well,' said the centaur god. 'But I shall expect you to do a lot of chores for me in return. And no more missing lessons. You'll never learn to be a proper healer at this rate.'

'I'll do my best,' Demon promised, grabbing his sacks. He kept one set of fingers crossed behind his back, though. What if another god had an urgent mission for him?

The Iris Express grumbled at him all the way up to Olympus. Chiron had had to bribe her with a bottle of lavender-scented mountain dew before she would let Demon on board. Last time he'd ridden in her, he'd had the whole herd of pegasi with him, and they'd been a bit nervous.

'Nasty wet pegasus poo,' Iris complained in her tinkly voice. 'All over my nice clean rainbow. Took me ages to get rid of it. I had to swoosh through at least five rain clouds before the smell went away. What if Zeus had wanted a lift down to earth? Or Hera?'

Demon shuddered. He didn't ever want to be on the bad side of either the King of the Gods or his scary wife.

'I'm sorry,' he said. 'I promise it will never happen again.' He'd worry about how to get Keith, Sky Pearl and the pegasi herd back to Olympus when he had to. Just now he had more than enough to deal with.

Iris dumped him onto the green grass of Olympus with a miffed sniff and a flurry of sparkles. 'Make sure it doesn't,' she said, before disappearing again.

Demon picked himself up and started to run towards the stables and the hospital shed where Arnie was in quarantine, and, he hoped, still asleep under the spell Demon had blown on his dad

Pan's silver pipes before he left for the Mountains of Burning Sand. As he raced up to the isolation pen, all was quiet. Raising himself up on tiptoe, Demon peered inside. There was poor Arnie, his beautiful golden feathers now totally restored, lying on his back, paws in the air, snoring louder than a dragon with a head cold. Demon slumped against the door in relief before running over to take a look at the stables. Everything was clean and shiny, and all the animals seemed content and well-fed, even the Giant Scorpion. Endeis, Chiron's daughter and Peleus's mum, had been looking after the stables for him, and it seemed she'd done a good job.

'Endeis,' he called softly, as he scratched under each one of Doris the Hydra's nine chins, making it drool happily. But there was no answer, so he dumped the sacks in his room and set off for Hestia's kitchens.

As usual, when he arrived the goddess's domain was full of steam and noise and good smells. Hestia herself was leaning over a large silver cauldron, stirring and tasting something beige and full of green lumps. As she looked up, Demon waved two large pots at her.

'I got them,' he shouted above the racket of clattering pans, and she beckoned him over, laying her ladle down.

'I am a goddess of my word,' she said, snagging a passing faun with her other hand as he handed the pots to her. 'Young Bion here will take you to the meat store – he'll be glad to get out of the heat. You may ask him for what you need for as long as the griffin needs feeding up. After that the beast must go back to ambrosia cake, like the rest of them.'

'Thank you, Your Divine Domestic Goddessness,' Demon said. Just then, a particularly delicious smell wafted past his nose, and his stomach rumbled like a volcano about to erupt. Before he could stop himself, he was licking his lips.

'Want a bowl of my new chicken stew?' Hestia asked. 'I've added some of Dionysus's white grapes to it, and some Sun Cow cream, but I think there's something else it needs. Maybe you can tell me what it is.'

Demon nodded hungrily, trying not to feel guilty about Arnie. He'd sicked up the food Antaeus had given him what seemed like hours and hours ago. The griffin wouldn't mind sleeping a few minutes longer, would it?

'It's delicious, but it needs something sour,' he mumbled through his third mouthful. 'Maybe lemon.'

'Perfect!' said Hestia, as Demon licked the bowl clean. 'Now off you go, Pandemonius. Shoo!'

Bion helped Demon to get a big barrowful of slightly green-looking minced lamb and a jug of blood gravy up to Arnie's pen, asking a flood of fascinated questions about all the beasts Demon looked after. When they arrived, the faun glanced around wide-eyed.

'I'd love to work here,' he said enviously. 'Out

in the fresh air. That kitchen's so hot – and I'm always burning myself.' Bion turned to go, then slapped his head.

'I nearly forgot. Hestia said you wanted these too,' he said, producing a glass jar of what looked like dried black insects. 'Though why anyone would want to sprinkle scarab beetles on perfectly good lamb, I've no idea. Sounds absolutely vile.' Whistling, he scampered back towards the kitchens, and Demon wheeled the barrow inside the pen, tipping it all out by Arnie's head, dribbling the blood gravy and the beetles over it. Bion was right. It looked and smelled revolting.

Demon got his dad's silver pipes out from his chiton, and stood just outside the pen door, which he locked firmly. He didn't know how Arnie was going to react when he woke up, and he definitely didn't want another finger bitten off – let alone anything else. Cautiously, Demon put the pipes to his lips and blew the wake-up call. First one golden griffin eye opened and then another. Then Arnie's eagle beak gaped wide and it let out a deafening screech that set Demon's teeth on edge and made the pen rattle. All in a minute, it hopped upright, whipped round and fell on the meat, gobbets of blood and flesh splatting on the sides of the pen as the griffin golloped down its meal faster than Zeus could throw a lightning bolt. Soon the whole big pile was gone. The griffin let out an enormous burp, sat down and began to groom itself.

'I see you put my feathers back, Pan's scrawny kid,' it said. 'Can I come out now? Only I'd like to stretch my wings.'

'Oh thank goodness,' Demon said. 'You're all right.' He opened the pen door and rushed in, so overcome with relief that he gave Arnie's big lion body a hug before he thought what he was doing.

'Ugh!' said Arnie, batting him away with a huge paw. 'That's quite enough of that.' It stalked out and spread its wings, flapping them so hard that the straw in the pen rose in a silvery cloud, making Demon cough and choke.

'I'll be needing more of that delicious lamb,

Pan's scrawny kid,' it called, as it flew towards Hephaestus's mountain. 'I'm still feeling a bit weak.'

Demon smiled. The griffin was definitely back to its old self.

3

BIG PEGASUS

After Arnie had flown out of sight, Demon went to find Endeis. She was with her friend, the nymph Althea, sharing the latest gossip about Zeus.

'He's spending all his time as a big, fat pigeon, cooing at some pretty princess down on earth. Zeusie's Eagle has got his feathers all in a twist about it. He's been forbidden to go anywhere near his master, in case he makes a mistake and eats him. I hear Eagle's so angry that he's pecked holes in all Zeusie's best sky robes.'

'Poor Eagle,' said Demon. 'It sounds like he needs cheering up.'

Althea sniggered.

'Well, if you really fancy getting your head bitten off,' she said. 'And Hera's on the rampage too. She turned all the beautiful passionflowers I brought her yesterday into little balls of flaming charcoal and threw them at the wall. She nearly set the whole palace on fire. I'd keep out of sight of both of them, if I were you.'

'Good advice,' said Demon. He'd seen Hera in a temper before. It wasn't a pretty sight, and he had no wish to tempt the Queen of the Gods into turning *him* into charcoal.

After he'd explained about baby Hygiea, Endeis smiled.

'Dad loves babies, though he'd never admit it, and he always grumbles about the crying,' she said. 'He was forever stealing Peleus away from me when he was tiny. If you need to help out with the baby I don't mind staying up here for a bit longer if you like, Pandemonius. Even with looking after the stables, it's a nice rest for me. Being Queen of Aegina is a tiring job, and my crown gets heavy sometimes.'

Demon thanked her and stumbled off to his bed above the stables. Within a minute of pulling his spidersilk blanket over him, he was asleep, tired out. His dreams were a confused whirl of maenads, babies and griffins.

Next morning, Demon was down at Chiron's cave almost before Eos had flung back the pink curtains of the dawn. A sleepy and rather grumpy centaur god greeted him.

'No wonder Asclepius and his wife wanted a rest,' he grumbled. 'Hygeia cried all night. She's only just stopped, and she still won't eat properly either.' Chiron rubbed one large, hairy hand over his red-rimmed eyes. Demon tried not to smile. Endeis had been right. It seemed a crying human baby could defeat even a god.

'I need you to go and gather some more bruise-flower blossoms,' Chiron said. 'Cut them while the dew is still on them, mind. You can take Hygeia with you. I'm going back to bed.' He thrust the baby into Demon's arms, and went into the very back of the cave.

'How am I supposed to cut flowers and carry you at the same time?' Demon muttered. He looked round the cave and spotted a big piece of the linen that Chiron used for making slings. 'Aha!' he said, wrapping her up in it and tying her to his front, as he'd seen the women in his home village do.

Hygeia's blue eyes went very round and she stuck her fist in her mouth, gnawing furiously.

Bleb! Gah! she chortled as they set off up the mountain.

A little while later, Hygeia was finally asleep in her cradle and Demon was tiptoeing around putting the last of the bruise-flowers out to dry on racks, when he heard the whoosh of wings, and urgent whinnying. He turned round to see the whole herd of pegasi swooping down outside the cave.

'Dehehehemon!' neighed Keith. 'On my back! Quick!'

Demon rushed outside, flapping his hands frantically.

'Shh!' he whispered. 'Sleeping baby!' Then he looked about nervously. Had the maenads returned? He relaxed a little as he saw nothing. 'What's the matter, Keith?'

'Hurry, you'll seeheehee! Bring your medicine sack!'

Demon ran to the back of the cave. Chiron's eyes flickered open as Demon knocked gently on the rocky wall.

'There's something wrong,' he said. 'But . . . Hygeia . . .'

'I heard,' Chiron said – and Demon remembered with relief that the centaur god could understand horse talk. 'Go quickly. It sounds urgent. I'll take care of the baby.'

Grabbing his emergency supplies, Demon sped out and vaulted onto Keith's back. With a rush of wings, they took off, swerving through the trees so that Demon had to duck or be swept off by slashing branches. A short time later, they landed by the waterfall where Demon had last met his dad, Pan. Standing right in the middle of the sunny glade was a gigantic white winged horse, at least five times as big as Keith. It was breathing hard, ears flat back against its skull, with terrible stripes of burned flesh underneath its belly and along its flanks. The horse's head hung low, and it was clearly in great distress. As Demon got off Keith's back, the small pegasi crowded round their big cousin, making unhappy little whinnies.

'Oh, you poor thing! Whatever happened?' Demon asked.

'Chimera,' neighed Big Pegasus. 'Bellerophon made me fly down so he could attack it. It burned me. I don't blame it, poor thing. I'd have breathed fire if someone had been trying to shove burning lead down my throat! But it *hurts*!'

'Let me help,' said Demon, calmly, though he wanted to scream at the thought of yet another horrible hero hurting one of the immortal beasts.

He knew just what to do for burns. Pulling a big bundle of green, fleshy leaves out of his bag, Demon slit them lengthways and laid them over the burns, rubbing in the sticky, soothing sap. Big Pegasus nuzzled him with his velvety muzzle in thanks.

'That should help for now,' Demon said. 'Let's go back to the cave, so we can put some proper dressings on them.'

'Just a moment!' said Big Pegasus. He craned his neck round, getting hold of his long, flowing tail with his teeth and pulling. He spat several long shining white hairs at Demon's feet. 'A small thank you, for your help. Tie those around your wrist, young healer. If you are ever in real danger, call me three times. I will know it, and come to your aid if I can.' He breathed on the tail hairs as Demon wound them round and round. They glowed slightly gold and knotted themselves together into a bracelet. It was beautiful, but Demon wondered if Chiron would approve. The centaur god was a bit stern about him using anything magical.

Just as they were all setting off for the cave, they heard a shout behind them.

'Where do you think you're going?'

Demon looked up to see a fair-haired young man appear out of the trees. He was dressed in a leather breastplate decorated with gold, and in one hand he held the remains of a spear, half burnt away. In the other he held a silver bridle.

Rage rose within Demon like a tidal wave.

'Bellerophon, I suppose,' he hissed through his teeth. 'The chimera-killer.'

'You've heard of my amazing prowess already,' Bellerophon said, clearly delighted. 'Word does travel fast. But I can't stay to be admired. I need to get another spear, and then old Peggy and I have orders to go and fight some Amazons. No time to lose.'

'I'm not admiring you, and you are NOT taking Big Pegasus!' Demon said, stepping forward and pushing Bellerophon in the chest. 'He needs rest and healing. Go away, you big beast-hurting bully!'

Bellerophon just laughed scornfully, throwing

away his broken spear and picking Demon up by the front of his chiton so his toes dangled.

'Don't be silly, little boy, I have his magic bridle,' he said, waving it in front of Demon's nose as he kicked and struggled to get free. 'Peggy has to come with me, whether he wants to or not, don't you, my winged wonder?'

Already, Big Pegasus was coming towards them on reluctant hooves. With a snarl, Bellerophon flung Demon into the middle of the herd of small pegasi, who scattered as he fell to the ground with a thump, winded for the second time in two days.

'Don't worry about me,' Big Pegasus neighed, as Bellerophon quickly bridled him and swung onto his back. 'It doesn't hurt a bit now.' As they soared up into the sunlight, one tiny, white wing feather drifted down through the air. Demon picked it up and tucked it into his horsehair bracelet. It felt warm, almost alive against his skin.

'I'll get you for this, Bellerophon,' he yelled when he had his breath back. But, as another scornful laugh floated down from the heavens,

Demon realised he had no idea how. What he did know, though, was that Big Pegasus had lied to make him feel better. Those burns were never going to heal if they weren't taken care of properly.

When Demon got back to Chiron's cave, still fuming, Hygeia was wailing again, and a harassed Chiron was trotting up and down, trying to soothe her. He looked worried.

'She won't drink sheep milk, and I can't get much goat milk into her either,' he said. 'She keeps on spitting it up. I'm trying her on chamomile water now.'

'Maybe she needs something different?' Demon hesitated. He didn't really know much about babies. 'Maybe unicorn milk? Or I could ask the Cattle of the Sun.'

'Good thinking, Pandemonius,' said Chiron, as Hygeia let out a scream worthy of one of the Furies and threw up on Chiron's shoulder.

'IRIS!' he bellowed. 'One for Olympus! NOW!'

34

A rainbow thumped into the grass at Demon's feet.

'No need to shout,' said Iris. 'I was coming to fetch Pandemonius anyway. I've just dumped a badly injured beast up on Olympus, and Endeis doesn't know what to do with it.'

'It must be the chimera,' said Demon, grabbing his medical bag again. 'We'd better hurry.'

'Bring back that milk, and don't forget to write up your notes,' came a last shout from below, as they shot up into the sky, leaving the wailing behind. Demon quickly looked in his bag. Yes! The beautiful red leather and gold book Athena had given him was there. Big Pegasus and the chimera would be the first cases in it!

When they arrived on Olympus, Endeis had got the chimera onto the trolley from the hospital shed with the help of some of the nymphs. It was a strange-looking two-headed creature. It had a lion's head and body, with a goat's head set right in the middle of its back, huge udders, and a patterned snake's tail. It was lying entirely still, except for a wisp of greenish-yellow smoke coming from the lion part's mouth, out of which stuck the other half of Beastly Bellerophon's spear.

It looked very sick indeed.

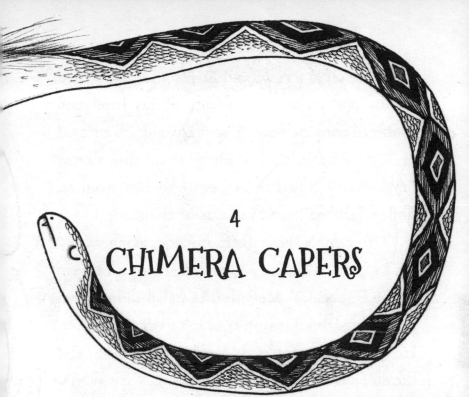

4
CHIMERA CAPERS

The unconscious beast lay on the table in the hospital shed as Demon tried to peer past the spear and into its smoking lion jaws. Its eyelids were twitching, and it was dribbling and shaking all over.

'It's no good,' he said to Endeis. 'That spear has to come out before I can do anything.'

Very gently, he took hold of the shaft and began to pull. Nothing happened, so he pulled a little harder. With an ominous sucking noise, the spear came free all in a rush, and Demon sat down hard on his bottom as it flew out of his hand and thumped onto the floor. The sharp end was encased in a red-hot ball of boiling lead, and almost immediately tiny flames began to rise from it. Endeis grabbed it and ran out of the shed.

'Oi!' came a shout from outside, along with a loud splash. 'What are you putting in my nice clean spring, Queenie?' Melanie the naiad didn't seem best pleased, but Demon couldn't worry about her. He had bigger problems. Lead was a poison, and the chimera had just swallowed a lot. What should he do next? He tried to remember Chiron's lessons.

In cases of poisoning make the patient vomit. He heard the centaur god's voice in his memory. Working fast, Demon rummaged in his medicine bag and on the shelves of the hospital shed, grabbing salt, chalk and some oatmeal. Then he frowned. There was something missing. What was it? A small pot of brownish powder caught his eye – that was it. Dried mushrooms! Quickly, he mixed them all up together with water and tipped the whole mess down the poor chimera's lion throat.

'Sorry,' he said, stroking both its heads gently as two pairs of eyes, one tawny gold, one slitted orange, glared at him.

All at once there was a terrible stench of scorched porridge.

HOICK HOICK HACK

went the beast, and then it threw up spectacularly, all over Demon. Bits of scorching oatmeal, smelly foam and burning bits of lead spattered him from head to toe.

'OUCH!' Demon screamed, and ran outside. He jumped straight into Melanie's spring, batting at himself frantically to get the burning bits off. Why oh why hadn't he put his Pyro-Protection suit on?

'Out! Out! Out!' cried the angry naiad, lifting him with surprisingly strong arms and flinging him onto the grass, before retreating into the water, snarling insults.

'Oh dear,' said Endeis. 'I'll try and calm her down. You see to that poor creature.'

Limping back to the hospital shed, with Offy and Yukus, the healing snakes in his necklace, already attending to the many blisters on his body, Demon saw ominous streamers of smoke pouring out of the door.

'Oh no!' he said, starting to run.

As he entered, the chimera gave one last *HOICK* and rolled off the table with a thud. Demon ran over to it, as it got to its feet, wobbling slightly.

'Thanks,' said the goat's head. 'That feels much better.' But the lion's head just growled and hiccuped and dripped chalky, mushroomy foam on the smouldering floor.

By the time Demon had put out about twenty tiny fires and got the chimera settled in a pen with two buckets of ambrosia cake gruel, he was exhausted. But there was no time to rest. Filling a couple of large flasks with milk from the unicorn and the Cattle of the Sun, Demon trudged back wearily to summon the Iris Express to take him down to earth. When he got to the cave Hygeia was still crying fretfully, and Chiron grabbed the two flasks from him eagerly.

'This'll do the trick,' he said, trotting back inside.

A little while later, as Demon was writing up his patient notes in Athena's beautiful new book, the silver pipes in the front of Demon's chiton began to vibrate. Then they began to emit a strident ringing sound. Demon dropped his quill, splattering ink everywhere, and clapped a hand to them quickly, afraid they would upset Hygeia even more. A voice sounded in his head. It almost blew his ears off.

PANDEMONIUS! PANDEMONIUS! He recognised it at once. It was his father, the forest god, Pan.

'I-I'm here, Your Dadness,' he said. What was going on? His dad had never summoned him like *this* before.

Come at once to your mother's house. She needs you to take care of some man-eating horses. There was an irritated grunt. *By Zeus's left eyeball, these satyrs are annoying. I must go and sort another battle out. Don't let me down, son. And hurry! Iris is on her way.*

The pipes lay still and quiet again. Demon rubbed his ears, which were still ringing. Man-eating horses? Where had they come from? And why were they anywhere near his mum? A baby's rising wail came to his ears, just as the Iris Express thudded down just outside the cave entrance.

'I'm sorry, Chiron,' he called desperately. 'My mum needs me. I've got to go!' And he stepped onto the rainbow and was whisked away from Mount Pelion with a *whoosh*.

'W-what's happening, Iris?' he asked, as terrible visions of his mum being torn apart by mad mares filled his head.

'No idea,' said Iris in a sulky voice. 'Anyone would think I'm your own personal transport. Pan's got no right to shout for me like that. I *am* a goddess, you know!'

'I know,' said Demon in his most deity-soothing voice. 'And you do a brilliant job, your Radiant Rainbowness. It's just . . . I haven't seen my mum since I went to Olympus and now my dad says there are man-eating —'

'Fine son you are,' Iris interrupted. 'Leaving your poor old mum to cope on her own.'

Demon went bright red and stamped his foot.

'That's not FAIR!' he shouted as it went right through Iris's wispy floor, making him lose his balance and fall down with a thump. Rainbow-coloured wisps whipped round him at once, tying him in place, including one over his mouth.

'Be quiet, Pandemonius, or I'll drop you into a wet cloud and leave you there,' sad the rainbow goddess. 'I've had quite enough of your chattering.'

'Mmmmph! MMMMPH!' Demon spluttered, struggling furiously, but he couldn't move or say a word. *It's not my fault,* he thought, furious. *The gods have kept me so busy I haven't had a chance to visit home.* But a tiny, guilty part of his brain wondered if he should have tried harder. How long had it been? He couldn't quite remember. Time on Olympus was strangely hard to pin down.

Demon had no more time to think, though, as

Iris's long, rainbow arms seized him by the neck of his chiton and dumped him like a naughty puppy onto the earth in front of his mum's door. As he got up from his knees, he could hear a familiar sort of wailing on the other side. He pushed the door open cautiously.

There was his mum, bending over not one but TWO toddlers, a boy and a girl, who were both bawling their eyes out. Who on Zeus's earth were *they*?

'Oh, Demon,' said his mum, looking up and rushing over with tears in her eyes to give him a hug. 'Your dad said he'd called you before he left. I'm so glad you're here. This is Ajax and Agatha, your new twin brother and sister. We've got to get them away. Those awful horses have already eaten two fauns and five of Old Demos's chickens. They're rampaging round the whole village now, trying to get into the houses. Listen!'

Mouth hanging open at hearing the surprising news that he had new siblings, Demon did as his mum asked and listened.

Just over the hill and coming closer was a terrible cacophony of neighing, along with the clatter of galloping hooves. Demon knew his mum couldn't understand it, but he could.

'Man-meat,' the horses were screaming. 'We want man-meat!'

5

MAN-EATING MARES

A freezing finger of fear slid down Demon's spine. His family was in danger, and he was the only one who could save them! There was no time to be afraid.

'Stay there, Mum! Lock the door after me, and hide! Don't come out till you hear silence,' he said, and dived outside again, ignoring his mum's distressed cries from inside.

There was only one thing to do.

Putting aside all the questions in his head about

his mum's new family, Demon pulled his silver pipes out and ran towards the racket. Four beautiful chestnut mares were rearing and battering their hooves against the neighbouring house, its earth walls beginning to crumble. Whistle-screams of terror came from inside, and Demon remembered that the blacksmith, Filippos, had two little girls.

'Hey!' he shouted, his heart beating faster than a rainstorm on leaves. 'Over here!' Immediately, the horses' heads whipped round. Their lips were drawn back over sets of sharp white teeth, dripping with bloody red foam.

As they began to pelt down the dusty road towards him, Demon took a deep breath and blew a massive blast on his dad's pipes. But still the mares came on, so mad and raging with hunger for manflesh that he knew they couldn't hear him. Demon blew and blew, but it was only when they were close enough that he could see their eyes that he tried one last desperate move – the new twiddle that his dad had taught him before he left for the Mountains of Burning Sand.

As if a taut rope had been strung in front of them, the four horses crashed to their knees and fell down, dead asleep, at his feet, strings of red spittle from their jaws soaking into the dust of the road. Demon stared, wild-eyed, at the remains of golden bridles on their heads as he started to put his pipes away. His hand trembled and shook, making it hard to get them into his chiton. That had been very close indeed! He wasn't sure that even Offy and Yukus could have mended him if he'd been chomped to pieces.

'Oh, Demon,' his mum cried, running out from the house, a twin under each arm. 'Are you all right? I was so worried! You shouldn't have –' But Demon interrupted her.

'Where did *they* come from, Mum?' he asked, pointing at the twins. His mother blushed.

'Oh, well . . . you know . . . me and your dad.' She stopped and cleared her throat. 'Me and your dad have been seeing a bit of each other, and Agatha and Ajax came along last summer.' She looked at Demon. 'I got lonely when you left.'

'Oh, Mum,' he said, and ran over to hug her and the twins. 'I'm sorry I haven't been home, it's just . . .'

'I know,' she said, laughing. 'Your dad told me all about it. You've been busy with those beasts of yours. And being Chiron's apprentice.' Her voice went a bit wobbly. 'We're so proud of you, son.'

'Ee-on,' said Ajax, pointing at Demon.

'Oss,' said Agatha, pointing at the four beasts on the ground.

'Ahem!' said a deep voice behind them. Demon turned round. Filippos the blacksmith and his wife, Hekuba, were standing there with large hammers over their shoulders, while their daughters stared at the horses with wide, round eyes.

'What are you going to do with them now you've knocked them out cold, lad?' Filippos asked.

'Take them up to Olympus,' Demon said. 'If I can get them onto the Iris Express.' *If Iris will even come and get me,* he thought. Hekuba tapped him on the shoulder as the other villagers straggled down the dusty road and began to crowd round the unconscious beasts, staring and exclaiming.

'Begging your mum's pardon, but we leave the gods alone, and they leave us alone, except on the big festival days at the temple, of course,' she said, eyeing the blue sky above, and gripping her hammer more tightly. 'They live up there, and we live down here, and that's how we like it. We don't want no Iris Express here.'

The villagers murmured nervously in agreement.

Demon understood. He'd felt much the same when he'd first got to Olympus.

'Don't worry,' he said. 'It'll only take a moment, then we'll be gone.' He frowned, looking down at the unconscious mares. 'How did these four get here anyway?'

There was a chorus of replies.

'It was that hero!'

'Ran off, he did.'

'That Heracles had no business leaving them tied up here,' said Filippos, his big voice booming out over the noisy crowd. 'They bit through their ropes in no time, even though they were made of gold.'

'Heracles,' said Demon, clenching his fists. 'HERACLES was here? Where is he, the beastly bully?' He peered around as if Heracles might be hiding under a bush.

'Said King Eurystheus didn't want them,' said Hekuba. 'He just hid in that big old jar of his when he saw their teeth. So Heracles told us he was off to find a new home for them and he'd be back soon. But it's been a whole day, so I reckon he's just dumped them on us. Just wait till I see that wretched hero again – I'll give him a taste of this!' She shook her hammer in the air.

'Never mind that silly hero,' said Demon's mum, stopping Agatha from crawling up to explore a chestnut mane. 'He's not coming back, and Demon needs our help.' She turned to him. 'Call your Iris Express and we'll all help lift the horses on for you. The sooner they're away from here the better.'

The crowd oohed and aahed and chattered as Demon closed his eyes, his hand on his pipes. *Please, your Dadness. Let Iris come,* he begged silently.

'Iris,' he called softly. Nothing happened. The villagers were all looking at him expectantly. He cleared his throat. There was nothing for it. He would have to shout for the goddess and take the consequences.

'IRIS!' he yelled. 'IRIS EXPRESS FOR ONE BOY, FOUR BEASTS! OLYMPUS-BOUND!'

The rainbow roared down out of the sky, making the villagers jump back, murmuring in awed voices. Demon glanced behind him. They were all on their knees with their heads bowed, even Hekuba.

'Now *that's* the kind of reception I like,' purred Iris. The villagers all gasped. Demon supposed it was strange to hear a rainbow talk, even if she was really a goddess. 'You could learn a thing or two from these good people, Pandemonius,' she said, her tone changing.

'I'm very sorry, Iris,' Demon said. 'But we do

need to get these four mares up to Olympus. They can't stay down here.'

'If there's even one tiny bit of horse poo anywhere near me when we land, I will drop you into Hephaestus's volcano, I really will.'

'There won't be, I promise,' said Demon, crossing his fingers. Surely horses didn't poo when they were asleep. Did they?

Iris snorted. She didn't sound convinced.

A team of willing but slightly scared villagers, headed by Filippos and Hekuba, hauled the four mares on board the rainbow.

'Don't leave it till there's another emergency,' said Demon's mum, giving him a hug.

Demon felt a bumpy lump fill his throat, so it was hard to speak.

'I wish I could stay longer,' he said, as the twins began to wail. 'I'll come back to visit as soon as I can.'

'I know you will, son. Now go and sort out those beasts. Try not to get eaten.'

He smiled, the corners of his mouth a little

wobbly. It was hard to leave his mum again, but he had no choice.

'I'll do my best,' he said, stepping onto the rainbow. 'Bye, Mum!'

The four mares lay on the grass, still sleeping. Iris had used her rainbow arms to roll them out as gently as she could, and now it was up to Demon to deal with them. He stood, looking down at the big beasts, wondering where to put them – and how to get them to the stables. If he woke them up they'd start eating the nymphs, or the other beasts, and he couldn't have that. He couldn't ask Hestia for any more meat, either. Getting that lamb for Arnie had been hard enough.

'What am I going to do?' he said aloud.

'Do about what?' said a cheerful and familiar voice behind him. It was Hermes, god of thieves and mischievous messenger to the gods. As Demon explained his problem, Hermes frowned and scratched his head.

'I see your point, young Pandemonius. Can't

have them eating the nymphs, and certainly not the gods,' he said. Demon shuddered. He hadn't even thought of the gods being eaten. What sort of trouble would he be in if they took a chunk out of Hera?

'What you really need is for them to act like normal horses,' said the god.

Demon nodded. 'But how –'

'Don't worry,' said Hermes, his white teeth flashing in a godly grin. 'I've just had one of my more brilliant ideas! Hang on – I'll be back in two shakes of a nymph's polishing cloth.' He clapped his invisibility hat on his head and disappeared.

Before Demon had had time to do more than open his mouth to ask where Hermes was going, the messenger god was back. Beside him stood a strange being, all long thin arms and legs, and eyes like pools of deep water. It seemed to be wrapped in a cloak made of darkness and shadows, and in its hand it bore a torch of black and gold flame.

'Pandemonius, meet Morpheus. Morpheus, meet Pandemonius,' Hermes said.

'Delighted,' said the being in a soft, soothing voice that made Demon want to curl up under his spidersilk blanket and sleep forever. Demon's eyelids drooped, and his mouth opened in an enormous yawn as he sank to the ground. Who on Olympus was Morpheus? And how could . . . he . . . help?

6

PSYCHE'S PROMISE

A blast of icy air hit Demon in the face. 'Wha—'
he spluttered, eyelashes thick with frost, as he
floated up from a dream of honeycakes.

'Wake up,' said Hermes irritably, as Demon sat
up with a jerk. The shadowy being was still
standing there.

'What happened?' Demon asked, wrapping his
arms round himself to get warm.

'You fell asleep,' said the god. 'Morpheus has

that effect on people. He's the spirit of dreams. I've protected you now, so it shouldn't happen again.'

Demon's tummy rumbled loudly. He looked at Morpheus.

'Was that you, putting honeycakes in my dream?' he asked the spirit. 'Now I'm starving.'

Morpheus laughed. It sounded like a bell tolling.

'I only work with what's there already,' he said. 'Now, what is your desire?'

Demon gestured to the four sleeping beasts.

'I need to make these four act like normal horses,' he said. 'At the moment all they want to do is eat everyone.' He frowned. 'But I still don't see how Hermes thinks you can help.'

'Who better than I?' Morpheus asked. 'Who else can reach deep into their heads and give them permanent dreams of hay and peace?'

Demon stared at the spirit. 'Can you really?' he asked.

Morpheus nodded.

'There will be a price,' he warned.

Demon stifled a sigh. There always seemed to be a price.

'Well, as long as it's not turning me into charcoal,' he said. 'What do I have to do?'

The spirit reached inside his billowing shadow cloak and pulled out a shiny, black crystal.

'This is a dreamcatcher,' he said, handing it to Demon. 'You will keep it with you always, for the next year, and at the end of that time I shall come to collect it. Everything you have dreamed, good or bad, will be inside it.'

Demon looked at the crystal. It seemed to have rainbows moving around deep within it, and it felt curiously squidgy.

'What will you use it for?' he asked.

'Mending the holes in my cloak,' said Morpheus, spreading it out to show ragged holes in the shadows. 'The nightmares tear at it, you see.'

'All right then.' Demon tucked the crystal in beside his dad's pipes, as Morpheus bent over the mares, whispering in their ears as he stroked his torch over their heads. Demon stepped forward, but Hermes held him back.

'Don't interfere,' he said quietly. 'They won't be burned. Morpheus carries only cold flame.'

As Demon watched, the mares relaxed visibly, going limp as wet seaweed. Morpheus beckoned to him.

'Play your pipes,' he whispered. 'Wake them.'

Demon pulled out his pipes for the second time that day, and blew the wake-up call, praying to every god and goddess on Olympus that whatever Morpheus had done had worked. Slowly, sleepily, the mares' eyes opened. Morpheus waved his torch in front of them in a strange rhythmic movement, murmuring and swaying gently in a way that made Demon want to go to sleep again.

'Keep playing and don't look,' said Hermes. So Demon did, keeping his eyes firmly fixed on their sixteen hooves. Suddenly, with a scramble of legs, the four mares heaved themselves to their feet.

Demon took in a sharp breath, making the pipes squeal horribly.

'You can stop now,' said Morpheus. 'They're fine.' Slowly, the mares came over to Demon on wobbly legs. They lipped at his arms gently.

'Hello,' they whinnied. 'Who are you? We're Swift, Shining, Yellow and Terrible. Where's the hay? We're hungry.'

'Follow me,' Demon said, letting out the breath he'd been holding with a whoosh. 'And welcome to Olympus.'

Having said goodbye to Hermes and Morpheus and thanked them, Demon settled the mares into stalls in the stables, and gave them each a pile of sun hay to munch on. But he soon noticed they were having difficulty eating with their pointed teeth. He fetched a rasp from the cupboard.

'I think I need to file those down a bit,' he said. As he worked, the mares told him their story.

'Our master, King Diomedes, was a cruel giant,' Swift told him. 'We were born hungry, and he starved us till we would have eaten anything. Then he filed our teeth sharp. He bound us to bronze mangers, and fed us criminals and traitors till blood and manflesh were the only things we could think about. After years and years, Heracles came. He killed our master and freed us, but then he tied our mouths up with golden bridles and ropes, and dragged us before some silly king who hid himself away in a big jar. But the king didn't seem to want us, so Heracles dragged us away again and tied us to trees in that village where you found us.'

'He beat us with whips,' neighed Terrible. 'We tried to escape, but he was too strong for us. And then, when he left us, we were so hungry.'

Yellow nuzzled Demon. 'We're sorry we ate the fauns.'

'And the chickens,' whinnied Shining.

Demon leaned against Yellow, almost unable to speak for the anger that filled him when he even thought about everyone who had mistreated the mares.

'Doesn't matter,' he said gruffly. 'You're here now. You're safe.'

He stumbled out of the stables, his fists clenched. How dare Diomedes turn those horses into meat-eaters? How dare Horrible Heracles tie them up and beat them? What had they ever done to him? Demon walked towards a little grove of trees, needing some peace and quiet to calm down by himself.

'One day I'll get even with you, Heracles,' he growled, as he entered the cool green of the grove and headed for his favourite stone bench by a willow. Then he stopped. The bench was already occupied by a hunched-over figure dressed all in white and gold. He could hear muffled sobs. Oh no! It was the newest goddess, Psyche. Why was she crying? He turned around, intending to tiptoe away. It was never a good idea to be around an upset goddess. Dreadful things could happen. He put one cautious foot in front of the other, but he hadn't gone more than three steps before an imperious voice rang out behind him.

'Stop!' it said, sniffling a bit. 'Come here.'

Reluctantly, Demon turned around again, dragging his feet as he approached the goddess. Her black hair was all messy, her nose was bright red at the tip, and her deep blue eyes were swollen and pink round the edges. She reached out and grabbed him by the ears, bringing him up close, so that she was glaring right into his face.

'If you EVER tell anyone you saw me looking like this, boy,' she hissed, 'I will tell Aphrodite you put beast poo in her nightie drawer.'

Demon blinked. As goddess threats went, he'd had worse.

'I won't, Your Divine Weepiness. I promise,' he said, trying to back away. But Psyche's grip only tightened, and her eyes narrowed thoughtfully.

'You're Pandemonius the Beast Keeper, aren't you? Pan's son?'

Demon nodded with difficulty.

'A little birdie told me that you haven't been

doing your job properly,' she said, an unpleasantly sly note creeping into her voice. At this, Demon forgot to be careful.

'Who told you that?' he asked, struggling to get free. 'It's not true. It's NOT.'

'Be silent, stable boy,' said Psyche, making a little twisting gesture with her hand. Immediately, Demon's tongue froze to the top of his mouth. She pushed him down on to the bench and stalked around him, intermittently sniffing and wiping her nose with a dainty lace hanky.

'I heard that a certain queen has been taking care of the beasts. And that you,' the goddess pointed a sharp-nailed finger at him, 'have been lazing about down on earth. I wonder how Hera would feel if I told her about that?'

Demon started to shake. It wasn't true, but Hera was not known for her patience, and he knew she was already in a terrible mood, because of Zeus hanging about down on earth with some princess, disguised as a pigeon. This was beginning to look very bad for him. He looked at Psyche, begging her with his eyes not to tell on him.

'I see you take my point,' said Psyche. 'It so happens that I need a boy who is good with beasts. I have to do one last tiny little task for Aphrodite. But I need the help of Zeus's Eagle, and I can't get at the wretched bird. I'm sure it wouldn't be a problem for a clever lad like you to persuade him to do what I need?' She made the twisting gesture again, and Demon found he could speak.

'Why exactly do you need Zeus's Eagle, your Divinity,' he asked.

All at once, Psyche sat down beside him with a thump, bursting into tears for a second time.

'Aphrodite won't let me marry my lovely Eros till I get her some water from the Spring of Eternal Youth,' she wailed. 'It's guarded by a horrid three-headed snake, and Eagle is the only one who can defeat it. I have to get him to come with me. I HAVE to!' She glared at Demon again.

'You WILL bring me Zeus's Eagle, boy. Meet

me here in the grove tomorrow night, or Hera shall hear of your neglect. You'll be a dung beetle before you know it, and then –' She stamped her foot and ground it into the dust. 'Squelch!'

7

THE MAGIC GOAT

Demon's mind was racing as fast as his legs, as he stumbled away from the grove. Who could he turn to now? He had no idea how to get to Zeus's Eagle. It lived in its own special eyrie at the very top of Zeus and Hera's palace. Who to ask? Hephaestus? No! The blacksmith god was too honest – he might tell Aphrodite that Psyche was cheating on her task. The nymphs? No! They never went near Zeus and Hera except to deliver flowers. Hestia? No! He'd asked her for too many favours already.

'Who?' he muttered, running his fingers through his curly hair till it stood up like a mad brush. Then he stopped dead. Of course! Chiron was Zeus's brother. Surely Chiron would know. He ran for the Iris Express, detouring by the hospital shed to pick up some of his most fragrant rose and cinnamon oil for her. With all these trips to earth and back again he needed to keep the rainbow goddess sweet.

Iris wasn't there.

'She's on a job for Artemis,' squeaked a passing cherub. 'Special arrow delivery. She won't be long.'

Demon paced up and down, as he waited, trying to think of a plan. But no plan came. Minutes dripped slowly by and still there was no sign of Iris. By the time the rainbow goddess arrived, Demon was practically dancing with impatience. Luckily Iris was pleased with her gift, and just as Helios drove his chariot over the horizon, Demon arrived at Chiron's cave again.

'I've orders to wait,' Iris said, but Demon wasn't listening.

'Chiron!' he called softly, just in case Hygeia was asleep. 'Chiron!' But there was no reply, only a deep humming sound. He tiptoed inside the cave. Chiron was rocking Hygeia in his arms. The baby was unnaturally quiet, and the centaur god's face was set in lines of deep sadness.

'Oh no!' Demon whispered.

'She's fading fast,' Chiron said. 'I've been waiting for you, Pandemonius. The milk you brought didn't work. She won't take her mother's milk. There's only one hope now. You must bring Amaltheia to me. Iris is waiting. Quick as you can. Even I can't keep the baby alive much longer.'

'Who's Amalth—' Demon began. But then he shook his head. He'd find out soon enough. His mission for Psyche would have to wait, whatever the cost to himself. Hygeia must be saved!

Travelling with Iris in the dark was a new experience. Her rainbow glowed around him, and Demon saw the stars through a transparent veil of colours. Below him shone the occasional glint of lamp or firelight, but the only real light came from the moon, shining full and yellow above.

'Beautiful,' he said, staring about him with wide, wondering eyes.

'I know I am,' said Iris. 'Glad you finally noticed.' He didn't correct her.

They came to a halt on a wild rocky mountainside in the middle of an island. Demon was baffled. Where were they – and more importantly, where was Amaltheia?

'Did you bring me to the right place, Iris?' he asked.

'Of course I did,' the rainbow snapped. 'In there!' A long finger of light pointed the way into a dark opening in the side of the mountain. Cautiously, Demon followed it in. The scent of thyme and rosemary rose from under his feet, but as soon as he entered the cave, he began to smell something different. A rank, musky stench, familiar as his own fingernails.

'Goat!' he said.

'Who are you calling goat, young man?' A

creaky bleat came from the shadows. 'My name is Amaltheia, and don't you forget it. I was nurse to Zeus himself once, you know. Show some respect.' Very slowly, one cloven hoof at a time, an enormous nanny goat emerged into the rainbow-lit dimness, groaning at each step. Her grey fleece hung from her in matted, tangled ribbons, and she was so thin that her ribs stuck out. On her head was a pair of huge, curling horns, which shone with a silvery light.

'Oh, thank Olympus,' said Demon. 'I've found you.'

'Who are you? And why do I need to be found?' asked the goat. But before he could answer, there was a rustling of straw, and something bright and golden leapt out of the shadows at him, knocking him to the ground. A long tongue licked his face, and an even longer tail beat a tattoo against his legs, small gold stars rising from it with every wag. There was a loud bark, and then a nose snuffled into his armpits, making him giggle.

'Get off,' he said, trying to struggle out from

underneath the hairy animal on top of him. He didn't have time for this.

'Yes, get off do, Golden dear,' bleated the goat. 'He can't talk with you sitting on his stomach.'

'Smells nice!' barked the dog, snuffling some more. He leapt off Demon, and padded away to sit by Amaltheia, panting loudly. The small golden stars hovered over his head. This was no ordinary dog.

'I'm Demon,' said Demon when he had his breath back. 'And I need you to come with me, Amaltheia. Chiron needs you right now. It's urgent.'

'Nothing is urgent when you're my age, young man,' said the goat gloomily. 'Why should I come? What's Chiron ever done for me? I'm quite happy here with Golden Dog, sunning my old bones and taking a little morsel of thyme and a little stardust when I fancy it. Which isn't often these days. My horns hurt, my hooves hurt. Everything hurts. No, my young friend. You'll have to find some other goat to help you.'

'Please,' Demon begged. 'There's this baby . . .' He explained about Hygeia as quickly as he could.

The old goat's eyes brightened for a moment at the mention of a baby, but then she was shaking her horns from side to side.

'It would do no good,' she said with another mournful bleat. 'I'm nearly dead myself. My milk is almost dry, and what would Golden do without me?'

'He could come too,' said Demon. 'And I'm sure Chiron would have something to make your old bones feel better. He's the greatest of all healers. If anyone can cure you, he can.' He crossed his fingers, hoping it was true.

Amaltheia snorted, spraying Demon with a fine mist of goat snot.

'Then why hasn't he done it before?' she grumbled. 'Or one of the other gods? None of them want me now I'm old. Even my little Zeusie hasn't been to see me for an age.' She gave Demon a sideways look out of her slitted yellow eyes. 'I could tell you a thing or two about him, you know! If I wanted to. The naughty boy!'

Demon's heart started to pitter patter. Was this the answer? Could Amaltheia tell him how to get to Zeus's Eagle? He got down on his knees beside the ancient beast.

'Won't you come?' he asked softly. 'To save the baby? Chiron says you're our last hope. He wants you, even if none of the others do.'

Golden Dog licked the old goat's ear once, very gently.

'Go!' he barked. 'I am!' Then, right before Demon's astonished eyes, the dog vanished.

'That dog!' Amaltheia said. 'Always haring off without thinking. Very well then, I'll come. But it'll do no good. I'm not what I once was, you know.'

When Iris dropped them outside the cave, Chiron was waiting for them. Golden Dog pranced around the centaur's hooves, wagging his tail so hard that a whole rush of stars shot out of it, settling on the grass stems like shiny pointy flowers.

'What took you so long?' he barked. Demon stared as he helped Amaltheia off the rainbow. Who *was* this dog? And how had he travelled here so fast? But Chiron was looking at the old goat and frowning.

'Oh dear,' he said. 'You are in a state, aren't you?'

'Well, hello to you too, Horse Man,' she said. Then she looked sideways at Demon. 'Your boy here says you can heal my old bones. Can you?'

Chiron sighed.

'I'll do my best,' he said. Trotting into the cave, he quickly returned with a bowl of thick white liquid, which frothed and bubbled. 'Drink this,' he told her.

Demon had never seen an animal gobble down medicine so quickly. Amaltheia practically inhaled it. She looked up, her muzzle dripping with foam.

'More!' she bleated.

Chiron smiled.

'Come in and lie down, and I'll mix it up right away,' he said. 'But first I've got someone here who needs you very badly.' As Demon settled the old goat on some soft fleeces, Chiron returned with Hygeia in his arms. Her deep blue eyes were very big in her tiny face, which was pinched and white. He laid her gently by the old goat's belly.

'Do you think you might manage a little milk

for her?' the centaur god asked, as Amaltheia nuzzled the baby's head.

'I'll try,' she said. 'But she's too weak to do it herself, poor mite. Let the boy help.'

Demon coaxed a small bowlful of milk out of Amaltheia, then started to drip the rich liquid into Hygeia's mouth with a clean cloth as she lay in the straw beside the old goat.

The first few drops of milk dribbled down the baby's chin and Demon felt a cold claw of fear grip his stomach.

'Come on,' he whispered. 'Come on, drink.' As if she had understood him, Hygeia swallowed. Almost at once a flush of pink ran over her face. She swallowed more. And more. And more. The bowl was now empty, so Demon tried to squeeze more out of the withered udders. But it was no good. Amaltheia's milk had run completely dry.

'No!' Demon said, as Hygeia looked up at him reproachfully. 'You can't . . .' His voice trailed off as the old goat slumped into the fleeces, her eyes closed. What were they going to do now?

'We must cure Amaltheia,' he almost shouted at Chiron, over the sound of Golden Dog howling. 'Hygeia needs her, and I . . . I need to talk to her.' The story of Psyche and her quest to find the Spring of Eternal Youth came spilling out of him. 'But it's hopeless if Amaltheia can't help me make a plan. Unless . . . unless *you* have a way of getting to Zeus's Eagle?' he finished.

Chiron shook his head, looking thoughtful, as Golden Dog gave one final howl and ran outside.

'I have as little to do with my brother as possible,' the centaur god said. 'His high-handed ways don't suit me. But you are right, Amaltheia is sure to know about his Eagle.' There was a grave look on his bearded face. 'We must try everything we can,' he said. 'I think it's time for you to fetch that magic box of yours. I don't like using it, but it may come up with a cure that will be ready more quickly than any of mine would. We can't wait till the next new moon to pick what I need.'

8

ZEUS'S EAGLE

Demon lifted the lifeless magic medicine box into his arms. It was a little dusty, so he blew on it.

'Atchoo,' he sneezed, as a cloud of fine grey particles rose into the air.

'Got a cold, Pan's scrawny kid?' said Arnie, poking its head round the hospital shed door. 'Where's that meat you promised me?' It clacked its beak in a menacing manner.

Demon groaned. He'd completely forgotten about feeding the griffin.

'Go and find Bion the faun,' he said. 'From Hestia's kitchens. He'll give you some.' The griffin flapped its wings.

'Bion the faun, eh? Sounds tasty!' He took off and soared into the air in the direction of the domestic goddess's realm.

'Don't you dare eat him!' shouted Demon. But Arnie was gone. Demon hesitated for a moment, then hoisted a bale of sun hay under his other arm and started to run. Every moment he was away from Hygeia and Amaltheia made the danger of them both dying greater. He couldn't risk it.

'I've got it,' he panted, as he rushed into the cave and dumped the box and the hay beside the goat. Chiron tapped the box with one great hoof.

'Unblock,' he said. Immediately, instead of the angry red cross Demon saw the last time he tried to use it, the box began to glow its normal silvery-blue colour around the edges.

'Hello, box,' said Demon, grinning. Although he didn't really need it any more, it was nice to have it back. He'd kind of missed it since Chiron had shut it down with a centaur spell.

'"Hellobox" not a recognised medical condition,' said the box in its metallic squawk. 'State nature of ailment.'

Demon sighed. Perhaps he hadn't missed it all *that* much.

'Very old, bald goat with achy everything and no milk,' he said, without much hope. The box lid opened a fraction and out shot two silvery tentacles, one with a trumpet-like attachment at the end, and the other with a set of sharp, snapping scissors. The scissors snipped at the matted hair and the trumpet roamed all over Amaltheia's limp body.

'Mind the baby,' said Chiron, grabbing her out of the way.

'Request denied,' said the box, as the tentacles shot back into it. 'Estimating symptoms.' It began to whir and flash, making a grinding noise.

'Extreme paliokatsikatitis detected by data centre.'

'Cat-sicka-what?' Demon asked, but the box was continuing.

'Also osteoponosis, galasterepsis and falakratitis,' said the box, in a smug voice.

Demon ground his teeth. He turned to Chiron.

'Can you make head or tail of what it's saying?' he asked.

Chiron shook his head.

'It's a mystery,' he said. 'Worse than useless.' The centaur god tapped the box again with his hoof. 'Do you have a cure, you infuriating thing?' he asked. So it wasn't just him that got annoyed by the box's weird language, Demon thought.

'Searching cloud for solutions,' said the box, as a small rainbow-coloured wheel of light began to revolve on its lid, over and over and over again. Finally, with a creak and a groan, it shot out a tiny bottle of bright green liquid, hitting Demon on the foot.

'Temporary solution only,' it said. 'Ailments incurable except by water from Spring of Eternal

Youth. Access currently denied.' Then the box gave a high-pitched whine and shut down.

'That,' said Chiron, 'is one of Hephaestus's more annoying creations. Still, let's see what it's given us.' Nestling Hygeia into Amaltheia's flank again, he bent down and picked the bottle up, uncorking it and holding it up to his nose to sniff.

'What is it?' Demon asked. 'Will it work?' His brain was whirring with excitement over the other thing the box had said. If water from the Spring of Eternal Youth was the only true cure for Amaltheia, he had even more reason to help Psyche get some. But first he had to wake the old goat up.

'Smells like strong extract of alfalfa mixed with another thing – algae, I think. And a touch of something else I can't work out. Can't do any harm to try it.' He handed the bottle to Demon. 'Drip it into Amaltheia's mouth, young healer. Only one drop, mind. Let's see what it does.'

Carefully Demon opened the old goat's jaws, pried her long, yellow teeth apart and let one drop of the green liquid fall.

Nothing.

'Give her another,' said Chiron.

It took five drops before Amaltheia's eyelids fluttered open.

'*Meh*,' she bleated, her nostrils flaring. 'Is that hay I smell? I fancy a nice bite of hay!' She looked at her belly. 'And I do believe my milk is back!'

With Hygeia in Chiron's arms and contentedly sucking away at a bottle, Demon sat down by Amaltheia and repeated the story of Psyche's task to bring Aphrodite water from the Spring of Eternal Youth by using Zeus's Eagle.

'Can you help?' he asked the nanny goat.

'Well,' said Amaltheia, 'since it seems that the eternal water is the only thing that will cure *me*, I suppose I'd better. Golden used to be friends with Eagle. I'll send him with you. He'll sniff out the way. He's good at slipping in and out of places.' She gave another loud *meh*, and Golden Dog came prancing in, his fur covered in burrs and grass seeds.

'Take this Demon boy to my Zeusie's Eagle, will you?' she said. 'But don't get caught by that

Hera. She'll turn you into a bone as soon as look at you.'

'Wait!' said Chiron, as Golden Dog leapt up on Demon, his big paws smearing his shoulders with mud. He reached over to a shelf and grabbed two stone bottles, handing them over. 'Eagle will like this oil for his feathers, and here's an empty one for the water.'

Demon tucked them into his chiton, turning his head to avoid a swipe from Golden Dog's long, wet tongue.

'Hold onto my ears,' woofed the hairy animal.

'Ugh! What?' said Demon, trying to wipe the dog slobber away.

'Hold onto my ears,' repeated the dog. So Demon took a soft, furry ear in each hand. Immediately, a dizzy whooshing sensation surrounded him. His stomach felt as if it was falling out of his feet, but even before he could draw a single breath he was standing in a white marble room full of gold-pink light. It was very high up, and out of the arched windows, he could see

Hephaestus's mountain. Demon had a bad feeling about this.

'Where are we?' he whispered. But before Golden Dog could answer, there was an ear-shattering shriek from the next-door room, a flash of light and the smell of singed flowers. Demon's knees turned to water. He knew that voice. It was Hera, the scary Queen of the Gods – and she was *not* in a good mood.

'Run!' barked Golden Dog, as the next shriek sent tiny pieces of flaming ash skittering through the door and across the marble floor.

Demon didn't need telling twice. He took to his heels and followed Golden Dog up a narrow flight of twisty stairs in the corner of the room. Round and round they climbed, up and up, until, panting, they fell out onto a marble platform, open to the air. Demon just had time to notice that it was covered in bloody shards of bone and what looked like a pile of shredded sky-blue robes before his whole body was seized and shaken by a gigantic beak, as enormous golden wings battered at him.

Zeus's Eagle was most definitely at home – and it looked like he thought Demon was his supper!

Demon stifled a cry of pain and fear, and then there was a long moment of chaos as Golden Dog jumped up against the huge feathery breast, barking frantically.

'Friend! Friend! Friend!' he yelped, as Eagle flapped and Demon was shaken this way and that like a piece of straw. Suddenly the chaos stopped. Demon fell to the floor and crawled to huddle up against the wall and count his bruises, as far away from the edge as he could get. It was a long way down! Golden Dog jumped in front and shielded him, the dog's tail a whirling mass of fur and stars.

'Friend!' he barked again, as Eagle soared out into the blue nothingness above, wheeled and flew in again, crash-landing on a massive perch carved out of a single piece of marble.

'What do you want?' the giant bird squawked, his terrifying golden eyes flashing red fire. 'And how did you get past Hera?'

Demon didn't dare to speak, but Golden Dog's jaws lolled open in a sharp-toothed grin.

'I can get anywhere,' he barked. 'And I wanted to see you, Old Beaky. So does this son of Pan. We need your help.'

Eagle looked at Demon suspiciously.

'What help?'

Demon quickly explained about Psyche, Eros, Aphrodite and Hygeia yet again.

'. . . and poor Amaltheia will die without the Water of Eternal Youth too,' he finished.

'That old goat,' Eagle said. 'Is she really still around? Well, I suppose Zeus would want me to help her, and it's not as if he needs me right now.' He bent down and snatched up a bloody bone, snapping it into tiny fragments with savage pleasure. 'Wretched god. How does he think being a pigeon is going to impress some silly princess? It was bad enough when he turned into a cuckoo for Hera! To be honest with you, I'm bored out of my feathers sitting here doing nothing, and I haven't had a good battle for ages.'

Timidly, Demon held up the little bottle.

'Talking of feathers, Chiron sent this for you,' he said. 'It's the oil he said you like. Shall I put it on for you?'

Eagle cocked his head and bent down towards Demon, who tried not to flinch.

'Perhaps I shan't eat you after all, Chiron's cub,' he said. 'But I warn you now, if Zeus comes back and finds me missing, I can't answer for the consequences for either of us. Are you willing to risk it?'

Demon gulped. He didn't really have a choice, did he? He had to save Amaltheia and Hygeia.

'Yes,' he said, despite the visions of lightning bolts and tiny clouds of ash and dust fleeing through his head. 'I am.'

9

MAGIC WATERS

Demon slid ungracefully off Eagle's back, landing in a heap on the floor of the grove at Psyche's feet. Golden Dog had done his usual vanishing act, saying he would meet them later.

'I brought Zeus's Eagle, Your Divinity,' he said. 'As requested.'

Psyche seized him by the arm and pulled him up.

'Does Zeus know?' she hissed in his ear.

'I can hear you perfectly well, you know,' said

Eagle. But, of course, the goddess couldn't understand him.

'No,' said Demon. 'Not yet. But we'd better hurry.'

'Mind my feathers,' said Eagle, as Demon gave the young goddess a boost up onto the great bird's back, and scrambled up behind her. The huge wings started to beat, and with a leap they were soaring upwards.

'Where exactly are we going?' Demon shouted, as he clung to Psyche's waist.

'The source of the River Styx, of course,' she shouted back. 'That's where the spring is.'

Demon's heart did a great leap against his ribs, fluttering and banging like a moth in a jar. The River Styx flowed through Hades' realm. He'd already been to the Underworld once, and he didn't want to tangle with the King of the Dead again. Not for anything. He never wanted to meet those terrifying angry ghosts or Hades' Skeleton Guards again either – he'd only escaped by the width of a griffin's toenail last time, even with Hermes' help.

But it was too late now. They were shooting through the blue sky like a lightning bolt, so fast that Demon didn't even dare to open his eyes for fear that they would be blown out of his head. He should have known that Zeus's Eagle would fly like no normal bird.

'WHEEE!' Psyche shrieked. 'This is fun! Go faster! Go faster!'

Goddesses! Demon thought, clinging on even tighter. *They're all mad.* But he didn't say it out loud.

Soon the pungent, medicinal scent of pine trees floated up from below, and the wind on Demon's face slowed. He dared to crack one eye open and found that they were circling over a looming mountain, crowned with triple peaks of crumbly grey rock. At its foot were endless evergreen woods, their dark tops waving in the breeze. Eagle tucked in his wings for landing and dived towards a small break in the trees. Demon saw a golden flash of fur below, and then he and Psyche were tumbling off into a gloomy glade, surrounded on three sides by gnarled and ancient trees whose branches were festooned with beards of hanging grey moss.

On the fourth side was a rocky archway, framed by crumbling blocks of stone. Demon squinted at the glowing green letters above it, as Golden Dog pranced and wagged around them.

'*Death's Last Sting Guards Youth's Fair Spring,*' he read aloud. 'What does that mean?'

'That!' barked the dog, running forward as a deafening hissing started in the darkness of the entrance. Six bright points of light blazed and flared, and then Demon saw it. A gigantic three-headed snake with diamond eyes slithered out of the cavern, the writhing green and silver coils of its body as thick as a hundred year-old tree trunk. It was heading straight for them.

Psyche screamed and hid behind Demon, who was frozen to the spot as Golden Dog barked and barked, trying to distract the creature. Then Eagle was in the air again, its talons reaching down to grab the enormous reptile behind the middle of its three heads, pulling it upwards and shrieking a wild, high challenge.

'Look out!' Demon yelled, ducking as the twisting snake tail lashed out towards them. Psyche threw herself on top of him, taking him to the ground as it whistled over their heads, missing them by the width of a Hydra's eyelash. Then both snake and bird were gone, up into the sky, with Eagle's battle shrieks fading into the distance.

Psyche scrambled off him, planting a foot right in the middle of Demon's back.

'Come on,' she said, her voice sharp and urgent. 'We don't have much time. Bring that dog with you.'

Demon rolled over, struggling for breath, got up, and staggered after the goddess. A horrible moaning and groaning came from within the cavern, making all the hairs on Demon's body stand up like tiny ice needles.

'Be careful,' whimpered Golden Dog, as he slunk along behind Demon on his belly. 'Don't annoy the ghosts.'

Demon stopped dead, just under the glowing green letters, one foot hovering over the threshold. A horrid memory of shrieking spectres with blood-red eyes and pointed teeth filled his head.

'G-Ghosts?' he whispered. 'What ghosts?' And then he saw them. On one side of the dark, damp cavern was a jostling line of misty grey shapes, all clawing at each other and trying to crowd through a single narrow door. Right beside the door stood a spring that oozed black, oily water like treacle down the rocky wall, and smelled like rotten eggs. That must be the source of the River Styx! As Demon tiptoed in sideways, trying not to attract attention, he saw that each moaning ghost held a small disc of copper, which it was waving in the air.

'Charon's obols,' he whispered. Charon was the terrifying old ferryman who rowed the souls of the dead across the Styx and into Hades' realm – but he needed paying. Demon stopped, feet turned numb with fear, but then Golden Dog's jaws gently gripped his wrist, tugging him on. Stumbling forward, Demon wrenched his eyes away from the ghosts, and saw Psyche kneeling by another spring, filling a stoppered jug made of pink glass and decorated with cherubs. Unlike the Styx, this spring bubbled out of the ground into a small marble basin, clear and clean, and shining with a soft, rosy light like the palest dawn. The Spring of Eternal Youth!

Demon knelt down and pulled out his own bottle, taking out the cork and slipping it into the basin.

'What are you doing?' asked Psyche.

'Getting some for Chiron,' said Demon, putting the cork in again, and ramming it down firmly. 'He told me to.'

'Well, don't tell Aphrodite,' said Psyche. 'She wants to be the only one to have it.' Then she gave Demon a sly look. 'Take a sip,' she said.

Demon stared at her.

'Wh-why?' he asked, too horrified to be polite.

'I want to see what it does of course, stupid,'

she snapped. 'And you're young enough that it shouldn't be noticeable.' But just as Demon was wondering how he was going to get out of this one, the goddess saw Golden Dog, who already had his head in the basin, lapping.

'Stop it, you idiot animal,' she said. But the dog drank on. All the burrs and tangles fell out of his coat, leaving it sleek and shining. He began to glow, and then, with a *poof!* and a strong scent of jasmine flowers, he disappeared.

'Oh well,' she said. 'I guess that answers that question.'

'What have you done?' Demon wailed, now too upset to be careful. 'Where has he gone?'

As one, all the ghostly heads snapped round.

'Oh no!' said Psyche. 'We need to get out of here – fast!'

Demon was already running. He dashed out of the cave and straight out into the unnatural darkness of a raging storm, with Psyche close behind him. Thunder crashed all around, and lightning flashed, lighting up the three peaks of the mountain.

Demon saw Eagle, his wings outlined with fire, drop the three-headed snake on the very topmost of the three pinnacles. Immediately the huge serpent began to writhe and wriggle downwards, back to its lair. There was no more time to worry about Golden Dog.

'Eagle,' he cried. 'Quick! Come and get us!'

But instead Eagle shot off towards the lightning. A piercing cry reached Demon from the clouds.

'My master calls me! Find your own way home!'

Frantically, Demon turned to Psyche, whose soaked black hair hung in ropes around her wet face.

'Eagle is summoned by Zeus and that snake is coming fast. Can you get us back to Olympus?' *Please!* he thought. *Please say yes!*

But Psyche shook her head. Her eyes were very big and her face was very pale. He'd never seen a goddess look scared before – but then Psyche hadn't *been* a goddess for very long.

'My powers won't be complete till I've finished my task,' she said through chattering teeth. 'I . . . I can only do little things. I must get back though. I promised Aphrodite I'd give her the water by the morning.'

Demon thought fast.

'IRIS!' he yelled. 'IRIS! BOY AND GODDESS PSYCHE FOR OLYMPUS!'

But Psyche was shaking her head again.

'Iris won't come,' she shouted. 'Aphrodite forbade her to help me.'

A particularly loud crash of thunder made them both put their hands over their ears, just before another sword of lightning slashed the sky open. Demon caught a glimpse of the snake, halfway down the mountain now. Its six diamond eyes were blazing like angry white fires.

'Look!' he screamed. 'It's coming! We have to get off the mountain NOW!'

Grabbing Psyche's hand, he started to pelt downhill through the pine trees, his breath coming in short, panicky pants.

Eagle had abandoned them, Zeus was in a rage and the snake was too.

How were they ever going to escape?

10

RAINY RESCUE

Every time the lightning flashed, Demon fought
the urge to cower down and burrow into the earth.
Was the King of the Gods angry with him? Was
Zeus toying with him, watching him run and run
until he finally chose to strike him down? Psyche
was ahead of him now, leaping over fallen logs like
one of Artemis's golden deer. Demon clutched at
his dad's pipes with one hand and tucked the little
bottle of spring water more firmly into his chiton
with the other.

'Please, Dad,' he shouted into the storm. 'Help us!' But there was no answer from Pan. He risked a glance over his shoulder. Was that a flash of diamond eyes in the trees behind? He held onto the pipes even harder. They were his one and only chance to stop the snake if it caught up to them.

But snakes are deaf. It won't work, said a panicky little voice in his head. He ignored it, brushing the stinging rain out of his eyes with his free hand. Something wet and tickly brushed his nose. It was the feather stuck into the horsehair bracelet Big Pegasus had given him.

His horsehair bracelet!

What had Big Pegasus said? *If you are ever in real danger call me three times. I will know it, and come to your aid if I can.*

Well, if this wasn't real danger, Demon didn't know what was.

'PEGASUS! PEGASUS! PEGASUS!' he screamed into the wind, his voice cracking on the third call.

Psyche nearly fell as she looked back at him,

her face screwed up with fear, stumbling to a halt. Then her eyes widened. She mouthed something Demon couldn't hear, and raised one arm, pointing, as she ran back towards him.

He whirled round. The snake was in sight, all three sets of jaws open and its six sharp needle fangs dripping venom.

Demon grasped his horsehair bracelet and called out one last, desperate time as Psyche reached him.

'PEGASUS! PEGASUS! PEGASUS!' he yelled, before he put his pipes to his mouth, ready to blow for both their lives.

'STOP!' came a trumpeting call from the heavens. Then the big white horse was hovering above, wings outspread. He landed between them and the snake. 'GRAB MY MANE!' he whinnied. Demon grabbed. With a dizzying whirl he found himself high up on Big Pegasus's withers. He leaned down to Psyche.

'Quick!' he said, holding out a hand.

Psyche landed behind him just as the snake caught up with them and reared back to strike. Big

Pegasus leapt into the air, beating his huge wings desperately. There was a rush of air by Demon's foot and a burning sensation as a drop of venom hit his bare ankle. The snake had missed – but only just! Quickly, Offy and Yukus slithered down his body, their own snake tongues flickering as they lapped up the poison before it could do any harm.

'Back to Olympus,' Psyche yelled to their rescuer.

Demon was too exhausted to argue. He slumped over Big Pegasus's neck, as they flew into the storm, so drained that he couldn't even worry about whether an angry Zeus was going to strike him with a lightning bolt on the way.

The winged horse dodged through the clouds, jinking and swerving as the lightning bolts flew around them. Demon gripped with his knees and wound Big Pegasus's mane round his fingers, trying desperately to cling on. He could feel Psyche shivering behind him as she clutched his waist tighter than a griffin gripping its prey. Gradually, as they flew higher and higher, the storm grew gentler, until, as they landed outside Aphrodite's pink palace, it had shrunk to a whirling mass of black cloud and noise centred around Zeus and Hera's palace.

Psyche slid down off the winged horse, her precious pink jug hugged to her chest. She put out a trembling hand and stroked Big Pegasus's velvety nose as she looked up at Demon.

'Thank you both,' she said. 'And I owe you, Pandemonius. I'll tell Hera how brave you were.' She straightened up, her face determined. 'And I'll speak to Zeus too. If I have to. But before that I must clean up and find Aphrodite. Now I have the water, she has a wedding to plan.' With that, Psyche turned and walked away through the pink marble doors to the love goddess's palace.

Demon wriggled into a more secure position and felt Big Pegasus flinch. Oh no! Had the snake venom got him too? He peered down, trying to see.

'Are you hurt?' he asked.

'Not so much,' the winged horse replied. 'But the chimera burns aren't too good.'

'Are you strong enough to fly me back to Chiron's cave? I can treat you properly there,' Demon said.

'Yes,' said Big Pegasus. 'My wings have been through worse than this.'

They soared into the air again, then swooped downwards towards the grey-green dot of Mount Pelion with its necklace of sand and sea.

As soon as they landed, Demon leapt off Big Pegasus's back.

'I'll be back to treat you in a minute,' he said, as he ran into the cave, then skidded to a halt, taking in the situation at a glance. Chiron was lying down, holding a sleeping Hygeia in one arm, and stroking Amaltheia's head with the other, humming a deep, soothing hum which filled the cave with peace. The ancient goat's horns had fallen off and her body had shrunk to nothing but skin and bones. The little bottle of green liquid was lying on its side, empty, and the whole cave was strewn with half-full bowls of herbs and concoctions. In the corner stood the magic medicine box, tipped over and with a huge hoof-shaped dent in its side. It was emitting a low whine, and a stream of crackling red sparks poured out of one corner.

The centaur god said nothing, but shook his head sadly, still humming. Demon wanted to cry. Had he gone through all this for nothing? Was he too late? No! Surely not. Surely that was a tiny flicker of Amaltheia's eyelid? He was NOT going to give up now. He would cure her. He *would*!

Demon ripped the bottle of water out of his chiton and took out the cork with his teeth. Lifting the old goat's hairy lip with his thumb, he began to dribble in the Water of Eternal Youth.

'Come on,' he muttered. 'Come on, old goat. I've been nearly cut in two by an eagle, chased by a mad snake, and made your Zeusie nearly obliterate Olympus with a storm. I'm in huge trouble when he catches up with me. I didn't go through all that for nothing. You can't let me down now. You have to live.'

He felt a large hand squeeze his shoulder.

'Time to let her go, young healer,' the centaur god said.

But Demon shook his head.

'No!' he said. 'It's got to work. It's *got* to.' And as he said the words, something amazing happened. It was as if Spring herself had laid a blanket of new health over the old goat. Her hair began to sprout, flesh appeared on her bones, and a brand new set of curling horns erupted from her head, silver like the rays of the moon. Streams of golden milk began to flow from her udders as she leapt up with a great *MEH!* of surprise, capering round the cave as if she was a newborn kid, sending bowls flying and milk spraying everywhere, before heading outside with bleats and leaps of joy.

Chiron let out such a roar of laughter that Hygeia woke with a wail.

'No more crying for you, little one,' he said, tossing her in the air and catching her again.

'There's enough milk now to feed a hundred babies, let alone a little shrimp like you!'

Demon was standing there with his feet stuck to the floor and his mouth open. Chiron clapped him on the back, sending him stumbling forward.

'Well done, my young apprentice. Well done! You've succeeded where your master has failed.'

As if the centaur god's words had freed him, Demon let out a whoop of relief.

'I did it! I did it!' he said, as Amaltheia returned.

'You did indeed, young man,' bleated the goat – no longer old, but young and strong again. She lay down in the straw, milk still pouring from her. 'Give me that baby. I'll take care of her now.'

A horsey head poked through the cave entrance as Hygeia began to nurse contentedly.

'Is this a private party, or can anyone join in?' whinnied Big Pegasus.

'Come in,' said Demon. 'And let me look at those burns. It's the least I can do.'

While Chiron bustled round, clearing up, and filling clean bowls with Amaltheia's spare milk,

Demon cleaned out the chimera wounds and bandaged them properly. They were deep and angry, and infection had started to set in. A blaze of red anger welled up inside him again. How dare that horrible hero let his poor steed get into such a state?

'How did you get away from Beastly Bellerophon?' he asked, trying not to grit his teeth.

'I left him snoring at the victory feast after we defeated the Amazons,' Big Pegasus said. His ears drooped. 'I'll have to go back soon, though. It was lucky you summoned me when you did.'

Just then, there was a whoosh outside the cave.

It was the Rainbow Express.

'Zeus wants you,' said Iris. 'Immediately.'

11
LOVE'S WEDDING

All the joy drained out of Demon, and terror filled him. He had once seen a giant jellyfish when he'd been with Eunice, and that's how he felt. All wobbly.

'Z . . . Zeus?' he stammered, hardly able to get the word out.

'Zeus,' said Iris. 'The King of the Gods. Remember him? You need to come right now.'

'Hold on just one minute,' said Chiron. 'What does my brother want with my apprentice?'

'I don't know,' said Iris. 'But he's summoned *his* Beast Keeper. And I don't want to answer for his temper if he's kept waiting for one more second.'

'Don't worry, Chiron,' Amaltheia bleated, scrambling up. Hygeia was full as a drum and sleeping peacefully, a dribble of milk running down her chin. 'I'll go with him. I've got a few words of my own to say to my Zeusie.' She trotted onto the Iris Express.

Chiron gave Demon a little push.

'Go on,' he said. 'You'll be all right. My brother likes brave heroes – and you're certainly that.'

Demon didn't feel very brave as he walked beside Amaltheia into Zeus's throne room. In fact he felt as if he was going to throw up everything he'd ever eaten in his life – which was not likely to last much longer, he reckoned. He'd taken Zeus's Eagle without permission, and those lightning bolts could frazzle him in an instant.

The King of the Gods was reclining on his

throne, with Eagle perched by one huge sandalled foot, gripping a bunch of lighting bolts in its beak. Small lightning flashes sizzled round him, and a continuous rumble of thunder was making the room shake. Demon took one look at the god's face, with its white beard bristling with anger, and fell to his knees.

'You stole my Eagle, Beast Keeper,' the King of the Gods growled. 'Explain yourself.'

Demon's mouth was dry as a dustbowl. He took a breath in and tried to speak, but no words came out.

'I,' he mouthed. 'I . . . '

Then Amaltheia trotted forward, and butted Zeus in the knee with her silver horns. Hard.

'Stop bullying the boy,' she bleated. 'If he hadn't borrowed your bird, I'd be dead, and then you'd be sorry. Ungrateful cub. I spend years of my life raising you, young Zeusiepants, and what do I get?'

She butted him on the other knee, even harder. *Bang!*

The nanny goat was really getting going now.

'No thanks.'

Bang!

'No gratitude.'

Bang! Bang!

'Not even a word on my birthday!'

Bang! Bang! Bang!

'I brought you up better than that! I've a good mind to tell your mother, Rhea!'

Zeus cleared his throat. The lightning fizzled out and the thunder shaking stopped.

'Enough, old goat!' he roared. 'You shall have the finest pen in the Stables of the Gods, and the best care from now on. Though I'm not sure my Beast Keeper will be available to look after you.' The King of the Gods looked over at Demon, frowning through his forest of eyebrows. 'Shall I bind you to my lightning bolts and throw you down to earth, boy? It's what you deserve.'

Demon was shaking now, a cold ripple of fear making his whole body tremble like an aspen leaf in a storm as he imagined smashing into the earth in a fiery blaze. He wondered just how much it would hurt.

Then Eagle spread his wings and soared up onto Zeus's shoulder, nipping at his ear.

'It's not his fault. I was bored,' he croaked. 'You left me all alone. Demon showed courage in coming to me – and he brought me nice feather oil too. You never bring me nice feather oil,' he finished, sulkily.

The King of the Gods threw up his hands in surrender.

'Very well,' he said. 'You are forgiven, Pandemonius, since all the beasts speak for you.' He reached in and stroked Eagle's head. 'You'd better come and look in on this creature occasionally, I suppose. Since he likes you so much. But never again take my Eagle without permission.'

Demon swallowed for about the fifty-fourth time, this time with relief.

'Thank you, Your High Mightiness,' he croaked. 'It was an em-em-emergency. I'll never d-do it again. I p-promise.'

Before Demon could say any more, Aphrodite arrived, her beautiful face even more glowing than usual, even if her expression was a little sour. She had obviously used the Water of Eternal Youth. Close behind her were Psyche and Eros, giggling and holding hands.

'We are to have a wedding,' Aphrodite said. 'With your permission, Zeus, of course.'

'Ah!' said Zeus. 'Our newest goddess Psyche. And do you really wish to marry this young rascal Eros?'

'Oh yes, please, Your Divine Majesty,' said Psyche, looking so happy that Demon almost didn't recognise her.

'Very well, then,' said Zeus. 'Aphrodite, I shall put you in charge. You're the best at weddings. Just make sure you consult Hera, though. It might cheer her up. She's not in the best of moods with me right now.' He got up and beckoned Eros closer. 'Actually,' he said in a very audible whisper. 'I could do with some advice from you, young Eros.'

★

It was the day of the wedding. Demon had scrubbed himself all over and was just getting into his best white, gold and purple chiton and his gold sandals when he heard a hubbub in the stables below. Fastening the last strap, he hurried down the steps. There, prancing about like a puppy, was Golden Dog. Round his neck he wore a wreath of pink roses, and a whole cloud of pink stars streamed out of his wagging tail.

'Golden!' Demon cried. 'You're back! Whatever happened to you?'

'I was running with the Hounds of the Heavens,' he barked. 'It was fun. But now you must hurry. Psyche has something to ask you!'

Demon trotted behind Golden Dog, across Olympus and up the steps of Aphrodite's palace. Psyche was waiting for him in the hall, with a crowd of chattering nymphs around her. She was dressed in the most beautiful gown, which seemed to be made of silky wisps of rainbow and mist, embroidered with tiny flowers made of sparkling gems. On her head was a delicate golden crown set with Colin's fire jewels, which shone like a living flame against her dark hair.

'Pandemonius,' she said, beaming. 'I have a job for you. Eros and I want you to be our ringbearer. Here!' She handed him a velvet cushion with a ring on it. It was shaped like a three-headed snake, with diamond eyes. Each snake had a fire jewel in its mouth.

'Isn't it pretty?' Psyche said happily. 'I designed it, and Hephaestus worked all night on it. Hera let him use some of her special fire jewels from the Colchian Dragon – *and* she gave me this beautiful crown. Aren't I lucky? I'm the only other goddess to have some! And Hephaestus says there'll be a special surprise for me after I put the ring on.'

Demon nodded speechlessly. He didn't know much about jewellery, but he wasn't entirely sure that *he'd* want to be reminded of that snake every day.

'It's, um, lovely,' he mumbled.

★

What seemed like hours later, Demon followed Psyche and Eros through a long arch of roses. A tiny cloud of cherubs buzzed overhead, dropping pink hearts and more rose petals over them. The smell made Demon want to sneeze. At the end, Zeus, Hera, Aphrodite and all the other gods and goddesses were waiting. Eagle was perched on the back of Zeus's throne, and Hera had a box of sugar rats open on her lap, which she was nibbling. She looked different somehow – not so forbidding. The Queen of the Heavens gave a ladylike hiccup, and one tiny pink bubble floated up out of her mouth. Eros had been up to his old tricks again!

As soon as the bride and groom reached the throne, trumpets sounded out of nowhere, along with flutes and drums. The happy couple knelt before Zeus.

'Where is the ring?' he asked, his voice booming round the walls, which were covered in a sea of pink and white flowers, all woven together with golden ribbons.

Demon came forward holding out the cushion,

and Eros took the ring and popped it on Psyche's finger. As soon as he did so, a pair of the most beautiful butterfly wings sprang out of Psyche's back.

'Oh!' she cried fluttering up into the air. 'I feel so different!'

'You are a true goddess, now,' said Zeus. 'Welcome to the family!' He held out a hand to each of them.

'Hail to Eros! Hail to Psyche!' he called out, and all the gods and goddesses called out with him. 'May they be happy for eternity together!'

Brightly coloured fireworks erupted all around, bursting with joyful bangs and crackles, as the newly-wed god and goddess led them through to the feast. Almost immediately Demon spotted Dionysus and his laughing maenads. With a shudder, he made his way to the other end of the long table, where Hephaestus was chatting to his dad, Pan.

'Sit with us, my boy,' Pan called, beckoning Demon over. 'I want to hear all about how you saved Carys and the twins from those mad horses.'

As everyone sat down, Zeus held up a hand.

'I have one more announcement to make,' he said. 'Step forward, Pandemonius, son of Pan!'

Amid cheers – the loudest of all coming from his dad – a nervous Demon came to kneel before the King of the Gods, who raised him to his feet.

'Psyche has told me of your great bravery. You are hereby promoted to Stablemaster of Olympus, and Official Eagle Keeper. I have also talked to Chiron, Endeis, Athene and Hestia. You shall have a permanent assistant to help you out in the stables when one of us needs you for an errand.' He crooked a finger, and Bion the faun sidled out of the crowd, looking quite overwhelmed.

'Teach him well, young Pandemonius. Teach him well! And now, let the feast begin!'

Demon couldn't quite believe his ears. A proper assistant! Now he would never have to worry that his beasts were being neglected again. He sighed happily and picked up a honeycake in each hand, heading over to congratulate Bion. This was turning out to be one of the best days of his life!

GLOSSARY

BEASTS:

Amaltheia *(Am-ul-THEE-a)*: Zeus's nanny goat. Not afraid to give the King of the Gods a butt where he needs it.

Basilisk *(BASS-uh-lisk)*: King of the serpents. Every bit of him is pointy, poisonous, or perilous.

Bronze Bulls: Fire-breathing bovines Khalko and Kafto, who were created by Hephaestus for King Aeetes of Colchis.

Celestial Horses *(SELL-ess-tee-ul)*: Giant stallions who pull Helios's chariot and the sun from east to west every day around the Earth.

Cerberus *(SER-ber-us)*: Huge three-headed, snake-maned hound, Guardian of the Underworld, and Hades' favourite cuddly pet.

Chimera *(Kay-MEER-a)*: Mad mash-up of goat, lion and snake.

Colchian Dragon *(COL-chee-un)*: Ares' smelly pet and Guardian of the Golden Fleece. Watch out for sparks if he farts . . . BOOOOOM!

Cretan Bull *(KREE-tun)*: A furious, fire-breathing bull. Don't stand too close.

Golden Dog: Magical and mysterious canine, with a tail that wags stars.

Griffin *(GRIH-fin)*: Couldn't decide if it was better to be a lion or an eagle, so decided to be both.

Hippocamps *(HIPPO-camps)*: Part horse, part fish. A sort of seahorse, if you like.

Hydra *(HY-druh)*: Nine-headed water monster. Hera somehow finds this loveable.

Ladon *(LAY-dun):* A many-headed dragon that never sleeps (maybe the heads take turns?)

Man-eating Mares: Bloodthirsty horses belonging to Diomedes the Giant.

Medean Dragons: Two poison-spitting, biting beasts that pull the witch-princess Medea's chariot.

Minotaur *(MIN-uh-tor)*: A monster-man with the head of a bull. Likes eating people.

Myrmex *(MER-mex)*: Giant fire ants. Like sun-worshipping and dancing.

Nemean Lion *(NEE-mee-un)*: A giant, indestructible lion. Swords and arrows bounce off his fur.

Pegasi *(PEG-a-sigh)*: Mini flying horses with cute gold horns.

Pegasus *(PEG-a-sus)*: Five times bigger than the pegasi. Bound to serve Beastly Bellerophon.

Phoenix *(FEE-nix)*: Wondrous bird with a burning desire to be reborn every 100 years.

Stymphalian Birds *(stim-FAY-lee-un)*: Man-eating birds with metal feathers, metal beaks and toxic dung.

Telchines *(TELL-keens)*: Underwater monsters with dog heads and seal flippers. Scary.

GODS AND GODDESSES:

Amphitrite *(AM-fih-TRY-tee)*: Sea Goddess and Poseidon's wife.

Aphrodite *(AF-ruh-DY-tee)*: Goddess of Love and Beauty and all things pink and fluffy.

Ares *(AIR-eez)*: God of War. Loves any excuse to pick a fight.

Athena *(a-THEE-na)*: Goddess of Wisdom and defender of pesky, troublesome heroes.

Artemis *(AR-te-miss)*: Goddess of the Hunt. Can't decide if she wants to protect animals or kill them.

Boreas *(BOH-ree-as)*: Icy God of the North Wind. Carries a handy bag of bouncy breezes.

Chiron *(KY-ron)*: Centaur God – part horse, part man – brother of Zeus and humungously awesome healer of all ills.

Dionysus *(DY-uh-NY-suss)*: God of Wine. Turns even sensible gods into silly goons.

Eos *(EE-oss)*: Goddess of the Dawn. Married to Tithonus, a grasshopper.

Eros *(EAR-oss)*: Mischievous young love god who likes playing with hearts.

Eris *(AIR-iss)*: Goddess of Discontent. Argumentative, likes war and blood a bit too much.

Hades *(HAY-deez)*: Zeus's youngest brother and the gloomy Ruler of the Underworld.

Helios *(HEE-lee-us)*: The bright, shiny and blinding God of the Sun.

Hephaestus *(Hih-FESS-tuss)*: God of Blacksmithing, Metal, Fire, Volcanoes, and everything awesome.

Hera *(HEER-a)*: Zeus's scary wife. Drives a chariot pulled by screechy peacocks.

Hermes *(HER-meez)*: Mischievous Messenger God with a handy invisibility hat and winged sandals.

Hestia *(HESS-tee-ah)*: Goddess of the Hearth and Home. Bakes the most heavenly treats.

Iris *(EYE-riss)*: Goddess of the Rainbow and messenger of the gods. Also a slightly sick-making form of transport between Olympus and Earth. Seatbelts, please!

Persephone *(per-SEF-oh-nee)*: Goddess of Spring, stolen away by Hades to be his wife. Made bad mistake of eating pomegranate seeds in the Underworld.

Poseidon *(puh-SY-dun)*: God of the Sea and controller of supernatural events.

Psyche *(SY-key)*: Butterfly-winged new goddess in love with Eros.

Zeus *(ZOOSS)*: King of the Gods. Fond of smiting people with lightning bolts.

OTHER MYTHICAL BEINGS

Antaeus *(an-TAY-ee-us)*: Superstrong giant and hero-killer. Collector of skulls.

Arachne *(ar-AKK-nee)*: Brilliant weaver. Turned into a spider by Athena for boasting about her skill. Oops.

Asclepius *(ass-KLEEP-ee-us)*: Healer apprentice to Chiron and the first ever doctor.

Autolycus *(AW-toe-lie-CUSS)*: A very naughty boy. Stole some cattle and blamed it on Heracles.

Bellerophon *(BELL-eh-ruh-fon)*: Beastly 'hero' who captured Big Pegasus and killed the poor Chimera.

Cherubs *(CHAIR-ubs)*: Small flying babies. Mostly cute.

Dryads *(DRY-ads)*: Tree spirits. Only slightly more serious than nymphs.

Endeis *(en-DAY-ees)*: Chiron's daughter and oread of Mount Pelion. Also Peleus's mum.

Epimetheus *(ep-ee-MEE-thee-us)*: Prometheus's silly brother who designed animals. Thank him for giving us the platypus and naked mole rat.

Eurydice *(YOUR-id-ee-see)*: Tree-nymph and all-time greatest love of Orpheus. Stepped on a snake by mistake. Died.

Geryon *(JAYR-ee-un)*: A cattle-loving Giant with a two-headed dog.

Heracles *(HAIR-a-kleez)*: The half-god 'hero' who was given twelve impossible tasks by scary Hera, including stealing poor Cerberus from the Underworld and dragging him up to Earth. Loooves killing magical beasts.

Jason *(JAY-sun)*: Fleece-stealing hero, basher of bulls and captain of the good ship *Argo*.

Lethe *(LEE-thee)*: Memory-stealing spirit of forgetfulness. Lives in a marsh.

Medea *(Med-EE-ah)*: Tricksy witch-princess, dragon-owner and girlfriend of Jason.

Maenads *(MAY-nads)*: Followers of Dionysus, lovers of dancing and partying.

Morpheus *(MOR-fee-us)*: Spirit of dreams. Sleepy sort of guy.

Myrmidons *(MER-mid-ons)*: Fierce ant-soldier subjects of Peleus's dad, King Aeacus of Aegina.

Naiads *(NYE-ads)*: Water spirits. Keeping Olympus clean and refreshed since 500 BC.

Nereids *(NEAR-ee-ids)*: Sea nymphs (girls) – their brothers are Nerites. Daughters of Nereus, the Old Man of the Sea.

Nereus *(NEH-re-us)*: The Old Man of the Sea, a shapeshifter fond of wrestling heroes like Heracles.

Nymphs *(NIMFS)*: Giggly, girly, dancing nature spirits.

Oread *(Or-AY-ad)*: Mountain nature spirit (see Endeis).

Orpheus *(or-FEE-us)*: Magnificent musician who tried to rescue his beloved Eurydice from the Underworld. (Massive fail there, then.)

Pandora *(pan-DOR-ah)*: The first human woman. Accidentally opened a jar full of evil.

Peleus *(PEL-ee-us)*: Chiron's boastful hero grandson and prince of Aegina. Likes swishing swords about.

Prometheus *(pruh-MEE-thee-us)*: Gave fire to mankind, and was sentenced to eternal torture by bird-pecking.

Satyrs *(SAY-ters)*: 50% goat, 50% human. 100% party animal.

Silenus *(sy-LEE-nus)*: Dionysus's best friend. Old and wise, but not that good at beast-care.

Tritons *(TRY-tuns)*: Half man, half two-tailed fish.

PLACES:

Aegina *(eye-GEE-na)*: Island ruled by Peleus's dad and mum. Home of the Myrmidons.

Aeolia *(ay-OH-lee-ah)*: Ancient name for Thessaly, an area of central Greece and bloody battleground of Ares and Eris.

Arcadia *(ar-CAY-dee-a)*: Wooded hills in Greece where the nymphs and dryads like to play.

Macriss *(MACK-riss)*: Large seahorse-shaped island off the Greek coast where Poseidon has his second palace.

Mount Pelion *(PEE-lee-on)*: Mountain in Northern Greece and happy home of Chiron the centaur and his apprentices.

Tartarus *(TAR-ta-russ)*: A delightful torture dungeon miles below the Underworld.

The Underworld: Hades' happy little kingdom of dead people, also known as Hell in Northern parts.